# THE WICKED STREETS

## Wenzell Brown

**Black Gat Books • Eureka California**

THE WICKED STREETS

Published by Black Gat Books
A division of Stark House Press
1315 H Street
Eureka, CA 95501, USA
griffinskye3@sbcglobal.net
www.starkhousepress.com

THE WICKED STREETS


ISBN: 979-8-88601-144-9

Text design by Mark Shepard, shepgraphics.com
Cover design by Jeff Vorzimmer, ¡caliente!design, Austin, Texas
Cover art by Howell Dodd
Proofreading by Bill Kelly



First Stark House Press/Black Gat Edition: May 2025

*Life on the wicked streets…*

"I know you're a square, Diane. But I thought you was hip enough to know what I am—a guy on the hook, a junkie, with hell always eight hours away. The cure—sure, I've taken it twice. But pretty soon something comes along that's too tough to take. A shot—just a tiny shot—and you'll be over the hump. You remember the way it was with everything calm and rosy and its starts building until you got a yen you can't control."

"But Buzz? He's not—"

"Not on the hook? Not yet. But he's hitting the weed hard and pretty soon there ain't going to be no bang left in it. So what's he got to turn to but the funk?"

"I can help him. I know I can."

"Quit kidding yourself, Diane. You can't help a guy like Buzz Baxter."

# 1

Buzz wondered if the girl would show up tonight. Maybe it would be better if she didn't. She was a cute little number, all right. But she was jailbait. Not more than sixteen. Maybe he ought to beat feet right out of here. But something about Diane had got into his blood. Besides, her old man was loaded with dough. Yeah, this could be a big deal if he played it right—a crazy, mixed-up kid with a gold spoon in her mouth. And she was nuts about him. So what was wrong with that? Why shouldn't Buzz Baxter cut himself a slice of cake?

All the same, he didn't like hanging around the entrance of the shooting gallery. The lights here were too bright, so that anybody could spot you. And there were some cats he didn't want to see. Besides, if you hung around in one spot too long the cops would start giving you the fish eye. They might even pat you down and tonight he couldn't afford that—not with the load he was carrying. But worse than that, Nucci might be on the prowl. And Nucci was one guy who really gave him the creeps.

Buzz decided he'd better step back into the arcade. It was just as light inside but there were plenty of things to duck behind, like the booths where you could take your own photographs or the fortune-telling machines. Or he could turn his back in case of trouble and pretend to be playing Ski-ball or Pokerino. He'd just started to turn when he saw Diane coming along the block. She was walking head down, bucking the wind, and she hadn't spotted him yet. Neat—that was the word for Diane. A real slick chick. Maybe a little too thin for his taste, but what the hell, you couldn't have everything. Besides she'd filled out in the right spots since he'd seen her last. The wind whipped the red raincoat about her, molded her rounded breasts and thighs.

She looked up and saw him and her face lit up like a Christmas tree. She came running toward him. He stood where he was, waiting for her. That's the way things ought to be, the dames rushing for Buzz Baxter. He grinned to himself. He'd have to play Diane just right, but this was one game where he knew all the rules. Act a little tough, as though you didn't give a damn, but create the impression you were holding yourself in, that you'd really like to fall all over yourself for the dame.

Just before Diane reached him, he took a step toward her and scooped her up in his arms. Before she even knew the score, he kissed her, his lips hot and hard on hers. He could hear the sharp intake of her breath and feel the tautness of her body. Then she yielded to him and her mouth was warm and her body clinging.

He straightened up and looked down at her. "Hi, chick. You're late. I thought you was standing me up. I was just ready to ankle along."

"Oh, Buzz, you know I wouldn't do that."

"No, I guess you wouldn't, at that." Her face was tilted up to his. A narrow, fine-boned face, with high, peaked cheekbones that gave depth to the hazel eyes. Her pale blonde hair was pulled back loosely. The neon lights above the doorway emphasized the whiteness of her skin and made the patches of rouge on her cheeks stand out in bold relief.

She was talking fast, telling him what a time she

had getting out. She'd had to wait for the old lady to go to sleep and then sneak away. He was listening with only half an ear. The rattle of rifle fire from the range in back of him was starting to get on his nerves. Why had he had to pick a goddamn shooting gallery to meet Diane? But he hadn't known about Nucci when he'd called her. Ever since he'd got the word this afternoon that the zombie had got sprung from Sing Sing he'd been jittery. Now, Diane was here he'd better find another spot, but fast.

He put his arm about her. "Let's get cracking, chick. We got things to do."

She clung to him and he found it hard to conceal his impatience. He almost dragged her toward the door. She laughed, "Where are we going, Buzz?"

He didn't know and for the moment he didn't care. All he wanted was to get out of the neon glare. As soon as he was on the sidewalk of 42nd Street, he felt better. The smell of hot dogs, frying onions, hot grease and pizza, the jostling of the crowd, the raucous scream of jukeboxes and record players all gave him a sense of security. This was it. The hipsters' paradise. The place where he belonged. Even the blinking lights of the second-run moving picture houses didn't bother him. They fell on too many faces, gave a certain anonymity to the crowds who filed by them.

He saw a darkened doorway and pulled Diane into it. He kissed her again, pressing his fingers hard against her back, rubbing his lips on hers. She didn't even try to pull away. Her mouth opened a little and he felt the roughness of her tongue. As he sensed her excitement rising, his own waned. This was going to be too easy, a pushover. He let his arms go slack and leaned back against the wall.

He said, "What'll it be, chick? You want to take in a jam session?"

She put her hands on his wrist. "I don't care, Buzz. Just so I'm with you."

Like taking candy from a baby, he thought. He pretended to think. "How you like your jazz, baby—hot or cool?"

"You'll have to teach me, Buzz."

Sure, and there were a lot of other things he'd teach her before he was through with her. He grinned in the darkness. "Hey, I know the spot. They got a five-piece combo that can really talk. Wait'll you hear those boys cut loose. They'll really send you."

She said, "Solid."

He had to laugh at her, trying to make with the jive talk. Just one look at her and anyone could see she was a square. He made his voice serious, a little doubtful. "I dunno, Diane. This is a hipster hangout, a real crummy dive."

She tugged at his arm and laughed up at him. "What are we waiting for?"

He kissed her lightly. "Solid, baby. Let's dangle."

**2**

Diane was scared, but she was excited too. Slipping out of the hotel tonight had been a crazy thing to do, but she didn't care. She'd just had to meet Buzz.

She thought of the way she'd first seen him, playing the piano at a fraternity dance. He'd been part of a six-man band, but the other players had faded out, laid down their instruments. Buzz hadn't even seemed to notice. His long, spatulate fingers had ranged the keyboard, beating out a hard, harsh rhythm. His face had been set, his eyes glazed. It was as though there were something he had to say, as though the ragged music were ripped out of him, telling the hurt and the anger that was a part of him. She had left her partner and crossed to the piano. Suddenly the angry life seemed to drain from Buzz's fingertips, and his arms had fallen limply to his sides. He'd looked up then and seen Diane. A crooked little smile had twisted his lips, and she'd smiled back.

But there was more to it than that. Something had passed between them. She'd gone out on the balcony and waited for Buzz, knowing that he'd come.

Even so, he'd moved up behind her so quietly that she had been taken by surprise when his hand slipped over hers where it rested on the railing.

He'd spoken softly. "Look, baby, I'm not supposed to mix with the paying guests. But I think maybe we got a lot in common."

She had said, "You were trying to say something back there while you were playing."

"Yeah, I was talkin' plenty. But I didn't think nobody'd catch wise. Hey, what about meeting me when the dance breaks up? That john of yours is tanked, but good. You could give him the slip easy."

He'd handed her the keys to his car and she'd waited for him. They'd driven around for a couple of hours before he'd taken her back to the school. He'd kissed her when he left, rough and hard. She'd tried to hold out against him, but not for long. He was alive and vital. He made the college boys she'd been playing around with seem pale and washed-out.

That had been at the end of the Christmas holidays and now it was nearly Easter. She'd written to him almost every day, though he'd answered only once or twice.

But now she was with him in New York, just the way she had planned it. She glanced up at him, smiling. The headlights of a passing car struck across his face. There was arrogance, a defiant pride in his lean, dark, intense features, in his flashing eyes. His arm tightened about her and his fingers bit into the soft flesh above her breast. She suppressed a little cry of pain but she didn't move away from him.

They'd been walking fast. They'd left the garish lights and the noise of 42nd Street behind and turned north up Eighth Avenue. The sidewalk was dark, stippled by the pale-yellow lights from all-night restaurants and bars. Buzz slowed down and she noticed that he looked behind him.

Her breath was coming hard. She said, "Buzz."

"Yeah."

"This place where we're going—"

He cut her off. "Look, baby, like I told you, this is a real fleabag dive. Maybe you'd like to go up to one of them hicty joints on Swing Street, so I'll lay it on the line. About fifteen minutes in one of them night spots and I wouldn't have nothing in my pockets but my hands. But it's george by me if you want to pull out. Just say the word and I'll whistle up a cab."

"Please, Buzz. I didn't mean anything. I was just asking."

"Okay, you want the name of the dive. It's the Green Elephant. But I ain't twisting your arm."

"Oh, Buzz, I want to go."

He grinned then. "Sorry I blew my top, baby. I get sort of touchy when I'm low on the dough. Anyway, the place ain't far. You can see the sign from here." He pointed along a cross street. Up ahead was a blinking neon sign, shaped crudely into the form of an elephant. Buzz stopped when they reached the entrance. "You sure this is what you want, baby?"

She started up the two crooked stone steps that led to the door with its black glass panel. The door swung open and the street was suddenly alive with the din of voices shouting above the wail of a jazz band. A drunk caromed into her. Buzz straight-armed him and held the door for her.

The room which they entered was long and narrow, illuminated only by tiny, naked ceiling lights. Men crowded three and four deep about the bar. The music had stopped and the voices rose around them, slurred, sodden with drink. The place was rank with the stench of stale beer and tobacco smoke. Mixed with it was another odor, at once sweet and acrid, which Diane could not place.

A man blocked their passage. He was dressed in a rumpled tuxedo of midnight blue. Diane stared at him, seeing the massive body with its wide, sloping shoulders, the round head with its heavy, blue-black jowls. He stared back, his hooded eyes expressionless until he saw Buzz behind her. Then his thick lips cracked in a mirthless smile. He said, "Hi, Buzz. You goin' back?"

"Sure thing. Who's around?"

The man shrugged. "Dottie, for one. And that trim is really climbin'."

"Is she alone?"

"No. Wally's with her."

Buzz took a step forward, but the man in the tux didn't move aside. He said, "There's something else, Buzz."

"Yeah?"

"Nucci was here a while back."

Diane saw Buzz's body stiffen. His tongue came out to wet his lips. "How long ago?"

"An hour, maybe. He was askin' for you. I told him you'd been around earlier but had shoved off. That you was headin' for some dive in Harlem."

"Thanks, Chip."

"Maybe he believed me, and maybe he's hip. Why don't you dangle, Buzz? Sit it out somewhere else. I don't want no hassle in here."

"You think I'm going to chase my tail because of Nucci?"

"You'd better, man. He's on the weed again and really wild. You don't stand a chance against a slicer like Nucci."

Buzz said, "To hell with that. I'm going back." He tried to push by, but Chip still blocked his path. They stood facing each other for a minute, then Chip stepped aside.

"Okay, it's your funeral. But don't say I didn't warn you."

Diane didn't understand. But she could sense the fear rising in Buzz in spite of his bravado. He slipped his arm beneath her coat and she could feel the coldness of his fingers on her skin. He led her toward the back of the bar, threading his way through the gaping men.

At the rear of the room, Diane saw a raised platform draped with flags. On it stood a battered piano and several other instruments left there by the band while they took their break. A second room stretched out to the left, which was even more dimly lit than the bar. High-backed booths lined both sides of the room and in the center there were half a dozen tables covered with grimy red-and-white checkered cloths.

Buzz grinned at her. "Here we are, chick. Them creeps up front won't bother us here."

Diane didn't know whether to be disappointed in the Green Elephant or not. It wasn't what she'd expected. It was too ordinary, too without character. She'd always pictured Buzz in the midst of bright lights and gay people, with him the center of it all. But she should have known better, she thought. From his scribbled notes, she had been warned that he wasn't with a band any longer, that he was having a rough time.

Buzz led her to a table. A girl was already seated there, sprawled in one of the wire-back chairs. The girl should have been pretty, Diane thought, but her face was gaunt and her blue eyes too big and glassy. Blood-red lipstick had been smeared on her full, pouting mouth, and honey-colored hair hung loosely about her neck.

Buzz said, "Diane, this is Dottie Marr."

The girl's lips twitched as Diane acknowledged the introduction, but she didn't speak. Her blue eyes were openly hostile.

Buzz asked, "Where's Wally? Chip told me you was together."

Dottie gave a little shrug. When she spoke her voice was thin, with a brassy quality. "He's gone back to the john to try to score. He's got the monkey bad. Can you fix him up?"

"Shut up." Buzz started to say some more. Then his eyes flicked to Diane and his mouth clamped shut.

Dottie said, "Wally's been gone a long time."

"Okay," Buzz snapped, "I'll go get him." He patted

Diane's arm. "You stay here with Dottie, chick. I won't be gone long."

Diane watched Buzz's lithe body as he strode across the dim room. When she turned back, Dottie was staring at her.

Dottie's voice was slurred. She said, "You act like you was really gone on the guy."

Diane was embarrassed. She looked down at her hands.

But Dottie's voice was insistent. "What's a fancy little twist like you going to do about it? Cats like Buzz only want one thing. You give it to him and pretty soon he's tired of you and kicks you out. You try holding out on him and pretty soon he's looking somewhere else for his honey."

Diane's eyes blazed with sudden anger. "What business is it of yours? Leave me alone."

Dottie's gaze passed slowly over Diane's face. "Cool it, sister. You ain't the only girl Buzz ever took a pass at. Maybe I got a stake in him myself."

"I don't believe you. Buzz wouldn't—"

Dottie leaned forward and patted Diane's hand. "Okay, believe what you want. But here's a little advice from somebody who knows the score. Forget about Buzz Baxter. Just take a nice long walk for yourself and never come back."

"I won't. I won't."

Dottie sighed. "Man, am I talking like a square? Just forget what I said. If Buzz knew I'd blown my lip, he'd bash my teeth in. So let's pass it all over. Let's say Buzz is a down cat. Sure, as far as I'm concerned he's perfect."

Diane started to retort but the girl paid no more attention to her. She was looking moodily at the full beer glass, the litter of candy bar wrappings on the table.

Diane twisted about in her chair searching for Buzz, but he was nowhere in sight. The bandsmen were filing back onto the rickety platform. A blue-and-white banner announced that this was Johnnie Lacy and his band. Diane watched them, glad for an excuse to divert her attention from the girl across the table.

The pianist slumped down at the piano. His fingers raced up and down the keys, striking out a chord here and there. Then his foot thumped and he gave a four-bar intro. The band fell in behind him, rolling at first, taking it easy. Then the drum picked up the tempo and the music swelled—hard, raucous, dissonant.

The instruments fell off, one by one, until there was only the sax, with the piano playing a muted counterpoint. The sax spiraled upward, twisting, ripping at the nerves, then flattening out on a white-hot blast of sound. There was a moment of silence and then the drum picked up a slow tom-tom beat.

Diane caught her breath as the torrent of sound poured over her. She sat motionless, as she had the night she first heard Buzz Baxter playing the piano. This was music such as she'd never heard before, and now she knew it wasn't only because of Buzz she'd come here tonight.

She didn't notice Buzz until he was beside her. He grinned. "Didn't I tell you those boys could put it out? Just dig that crazy sax."

Diane didn't answer. All she wanted was to listen to the jagged bursts of sound that seemed to beat against her. But Buzz was insistent. He said, "Hey, Diane, you remember Wally Jones. He was playin' with me in the band up at Tarymount."

Diane looked at the boy beside Buzz. He was short, with a broad face and kinky, brick-red hair. His eyes seemed to swim beneath the thick lenses of his glasses. She remembered him vaguely. He'd played the drums at the dance the night she'd first met Buzz.

Wally was swaying. He put out a hand and Diane touched it reluctantly, shuddering a little at the feel of his cold, moist palm. She thought he was drunk at first, then she realized it was more than that. Her eyes went inquiringly to Buzz, but Buzz seemed not to notice. He flopped down in the chair beside her.

She looked back to the bandstand. The music had stopped. The pianist got up and started toward their table. He stopped beside them and spoke to Buzz. "Hey, man, how we doing?"

"Man, you're gassing 'em." Buzz laughed and spoke to Diane. "Meet Johnnie Lacy, the cat with the educated fingers. If you go for progressive stuff, Johnnie's your boy."

Lacy chuckled, "Get off the key, Buzz. Your needle's scratching."

Diane was studying the bandleader. He was nearly as tall as Buzz, but built more compactly. His cheeks were hollowed out and there was an almost fanatical gleam in his dark eyes. Yet there was something steady about him, a set purpose, a quality of controlled urgency that formed a strange contrast with Buzz's reckless, willful good looks.

Lacy's eyes met hers and she glanced down. She heard him say to Buzz, "How'd you like a crack at the piano, man? Me, I'm beat down to my feet."

"Great." Buzz turned to Diane. "You don't care if the old maestro takes a turn, do you?"

"I want to hear you, Buzz."

Buzz grinned at Lacy. "I'll really show you up, man. The crowd'll be yelling for Baxter once they hear me hit those ivories."

Buzz took a few steps toward the bandstand. Then suddenly his body went stiff. From the bar came the sound of scuffling and the roar of Chip's voice. Then a man came to the archway that separated the two rooms. He stood there, spraddle-legged, with the light of the bandstand full upon him. Diane could see his face as though it were spotlighted, the long hard features, the skin with its gray pallor, the bloodless lips. But it was his eyes that really frightened her. They were pale slate-gray, the whites shot with red veins. Beneath the eyes were little pouches of puckered skin that made her think of the unblinking stare of a lizard.

Buzz swung around and came racing back to the table. There was panic in his face. He grabbed Diane's hand. "Come on, kid, we got to scram out of here."

"What's wrong, Buzz?"

"Don't talk, just move." His hand was tugging at her, forcing her to her feet. He pulled her back, away from the bandstand toward the rear. "For God's sake, Diane. Hurry!"

Somehow the frantic fear in his voice was transferred to her. She saw the emergency door at the back and started to run toward it, hearing his footsteps following close behind her.

At the door she turned to look back. The man was walking toward them, moving steadily. The shadow of his hat brim and the swirling smoke masked his face but there was something sure and menacing in his steady tread, in the posture of his lean body.

Buzz wrenched at the door, flung it open, and pushed

her outside. They were in a narrow black alleyway between two buildings. Buzz snatched at her wrist and she had to run beside him to match his stride.

"Buzz—"

"There ain't time to talk. Just keep going."

Behind her she heard the screech of the door. She pulled away from Buzz and looked over her shoulder. The door was opening. The narrow slit of light broadened into a yellow swathe.

"Buzz—" But he wasn't there anymore. He was racing down the alley, shouting at a cab that was crawling by the entrance. The taxi stopped, backed up. Buzz ripped the door open and jumped inside.

Fear made Diane numb, incapable of motion. Was Buzz deserting her, leaving her here alone in the alley with the unknown man? Feet crackled on the grit-covered concrete of the alley behind her. Diane caught a glimpse of a long, angular shadow silhouetted dimly in the light of the half-open door. Terror choked off the scream that rose to her throat.

A shout echoed blurrily along the alley. It took her a moment to recognize Buzz's voice. He was calling her name, urging her to run. She whirled and saw that the cab was still waiting, the door partly open, the interior dark.

Fingers slid along the sleeve of her coat, but she wrenched free. Then she was running, wildly, frantically, her high heels nearly tripping her. It was only thirty feet to the mouth of the alley, but the space seemed to stretch on forever. The thudding of her heart blotted out every other sound so that she was unable to tell whether or not the man was behind her.

The taxi door swung back and she fell forward, half in and half out of the cab. Her knees struck against the running board with paralyzing force. Then Buzz's arms were around her, drawing her into the seat beside him. She was vaguely aware of the door slamming and the cab jolting into motion. A block or so away it slowed down and the cabbie peered back at them.

He said, "What's going on here? You kids taking it on the lam from the cops?"

"Nothing like that, Mac."

The cabbie scratched the side of his head. "Yeah? Well, I dunno. I don't want no trouble with the nabs. I gotta know the score."

"Some zombie back there had a load on and was making a pass at my girl. So we had to beat feet, that's all."

The cabbie was studying them. "So you leave the girl back there while you go shopping for a cab."

"I got her out, didn't I? Was I supposed to make like a hero and get us both carved up?"

The cabbie shrugged, "Okay—okay. I'll buy. Where you want to go?"

Buzz gave him the address of Diane's hotel and the cab started wheeling.

Diane rested against the back of the seat. Her knees were throbbing where she had fallen; she wanted to cry with the pain. Buzz drew her close.

She whispered, "Who was he, Buzz? Tell me."

He silenced her by pressing his lips against her mouth. He drew away a little and his head jerked toward the driver. "Don't talk, Diane. Not here."

She closed her eyes and relaxed against him. His lips rubbed softly against the column of her throat and his hands caressed her. She began to tremble. Then he moved away. When she looked up he was not watching her. He had twisted about so that he could see through the rear window of the cab. Her fingers went to his cheek, stroking them lightly. He did not stir. His eyes remained riveted on the street behind.

**3**

The taxi swung into the curb in front of the hotel and came to a stop. Diane's hands went around Buzz's neck and she drew his face down to hers. She could hear the harshness of his breathing, feel the rigidity of the muscles of his neck and shoulders.

"Tomorrow?" she whispered.

His voice was strained. "Maybe, baby. I can't be sure. I got things to do."

"Please, Buzz. I'll be waiting."

"Sure, I'll try. You just sit tight, chick." His eyes flicked away from her toward the window again.

Her gaze followed his. Another cab had drawn up a dozen feet behind, its lights dimmed, its motor idling.

"What's the matter, Buzz? Tell me what it's all about."

"There's no cause to worry. A guy like me makes an enemy or two, is all."

"I want to help."

"There ain't nothin' you can do. Not tonight anyhow. So be a sweet kid and hop into the hotel, will you? I'll be in touch with you."

"But Buzz—"

"There ain't time to explain now. Get going, will you, baby?"

A spurt of anger passed through her. She jerked open the door of the cab and ran across the sidewalk toward the revolving door. She turned, half expecting Buzz to follow her, but his taxi was already in motion, racing down the deserted avenue. She watched until it caromed into a side street and disappeared.

Tears stung her eyes. So this was the end of her night with Buzz, a cheap tinsel dream with herself alone on the sidewalk.

She remembered the second cab. It was still there. Buzz had been fleeing from phantoms. As she watched the cab began to crawl toward her. She could make out the hunched figure of the driver, see a tiny circle of light from the cigarette of the passenger behind him. Her anger changed to panic. She thought of the drawn, gray face, the heavy-lidded eyes of the man she had seen in the Green Elephant. Was he in the cab, stalking her? She swung about and hurried through the revolving door into the lobby.

Wide, curved stairs led to the second floor. She chose the steps rather than the elevator. She didn't want to speak to the night clerk or the operator. At the top of the stairs she stopped to listen. She heard the clang of the elevator door and that was all. Nobody had followed her. She tiptoed down the carpeted hallway and listened at the door of her suite. There was no sound from within.

She turned the key quietly and entered the dark foyer. Her mother moaned softly in her sleep. Diane moved along the passageway to her own room. The lights from Fifth Avenue bathed it with a pale-yellow glow. She went to the window and peered out. The cab was gone.

She undressed in the darkness and pulled a nightdress over her head, but she was too excited to sleep. She went back to the window and stood watching the syncopated movement of the traffic lights, thinking of Buzz, still feeling the tingling pleasure of his arms about her, his lips on her mouth. Somewhere in the back of her mind fragments of music shaped and reshaped until they formed the tormented jungle rhythm of Johnnie Lacy's band.

A moving shadow caught her eye. She studied the archway of the church across the street. A tiny circle of red showed in the blackness. At first she thought it was a reflection of light, but then it moved slightly. A cigarette. A man in the arched doorway, watching.

The cigarette spiraled outward landing on the sidewalk with a tiny shower of sparks. Then a man stepped out of the shadow.

There was no mistaking the long, angular body, the wide shoulders, the narrow waist of the man she had seen in the Green Elephant. He shambled along until he was beneath the street light on the corner. Then he swung around slowly and raised his head so that he could stare up at the window. In the artificial glare his face seemed featureless, as though covered with a gray mask.

A shudder coursed through her. Then she remained rigid, fearful that the slightest motion might reveal her presence at the window. The man lowered his gaze. He fumbled in the pockets of his gray coat and brought out a pack of cigarettes. He lit one, cupping his hands about the flame of the match. He looked up again at the window. He hunched his coat more tightly about his shoulders. Slowly, deliberately, he started across the empty street at an angle, heading for the entrance of the hotel. Diane watched him until he disappeared beneath the marquee.

He must have entered the lobby. She waited for a

few minutes, but she didn't see him leave. She crossed to the bed and flung herself upon it, burying her head in the pillows. But the tautness would not leave her. She was listening for some sign that the man was close at hand, prowling the corridors. Who was he? Why had Buzz been so afraid of him? The questions kept chasing themselves around, giving her no peace.

The shrill clamor of the telephone startled her so that she gave a little cry. She ran to it and snatched it up. "Buzz! Oh Buzz!"

There was no answer, only the thin nasal hum of an open wire, and then a chuckling sound.

She asked sharply, "Buzz, are you there?"

The voice that answered was flat, toneless. "This ain't Buzz. I guess I don't need to tell you who I am." She knew all right. It could be only the man with the gray face. His voice rasped on. "It looks to me like you and Buzz is sort of sweet on each other. How about it, Diane?"

"How'd you know my name?"

"Easy as pie, sister. I trail you to the hotel, find out where you're shacked up. I pass out a little lettuce and ask a few questions and up pop all the answers. There's nothing to it. Nothin' at all."

"What do you want?"

"Just a little chat, Diane. Just some jaw-blocking is all."

"Leave me alone."

He gave a harsh laugh. "Don't feed me that, sister. Climb off your high horse. You and me got plenty to talk about."

"No."

"Listen to me, sister. You wouldn't want nothing bad to happen to Buzz, would you?"

"I don't understand."

"Maybe you don't at that, sister. So let me put it on the line. When a cheap punk tries to horn in on another guy's racket, he's likely to get hurt. Hurt real bad."

"But Buzz—"

"Buzz ain't no bargain, kid, but I'll say one thing for him, he's a pretty boy. But maybe that ain't going to last long. How'd you like to see him with his face all sliced up, a real sweet job done by an expert."

"No! Oh, no!"

"It could happen, but maybe it don't have to. It could be it's up to you."

"What do you mean?"

"Well, you're a real fancy frill, Diane. Yeah, a sweet piece of goods, just what a guy dreams of when he's sitting around in stir. Now if you and me could get close, maybe I'd be so busy I'd forget all about Buzz."

"You're crazy!"

The voice was suddenly loud, angry. "Don't pull that stuff on me, sister. I'm a guy that gets what he wants. And I want you, sweetheart. You want me to tell you some more? You want me to draw diagrams?"

The phone slipped from her fingers, fell to the bed. She heard the voice grating on but she couldn't distinguish the words. After a minute she snatched up the instrument and thrust it back on its cradle.

She stood still in the darkness, waiting, afraid that the phone would ring again. But it remained silent. Somehow she had to reach Buzz, warn him of the danger. But how? He had told her that he had no telephone and the only address he'd ever given her was a post office box. She'd have to wait until he called her.

She propped herself up on the pillows and flicked on the light beside her bed. She thought that she wouldn't sleep, but after a while exhaustion overcame her. Memories of the night fused into her dreams. The music of Johnnie Lacy's band rose shrill and raucous, then tapered off so that all she could hear was the soft tattoo of the brushes. The drums grew louder— became the sound of running footsteps, hers and Buzz's. Then another drum picked up a counterpoint. The foot beats of the stranger, soft at first, secretive, then growing bolder until they drove out every other sound. She and Buzz fled through a jungle of neon lights, shooting galleries, garish marquees of movie houses, pursued by the relentless pounding foot beats, too frightened to hesitate or turn.

She stirred restlessly, half awakened, and then returned to her dreams.

4

Buzz ducked into the subway; he'd paid the taxi driver off in front of the kiosk. He'd have liked to take the cab right back to his pad, but that wasn't in the cards. Once he'd bought his subway token, he'd have only a dime in the world to bless himself with.

At the foot of the subway stairs he looked around furtively. Nobody seemed to be following him. All the same he'd better watch his step. There was no sense taking any chances, not when you had a guy like Nucci on your tail. He felt cold sweat break out over his forehead just thinking about Nucci. That was one real crazy cat, a slicer, a right handy guy with a knife.

Yeah, he'd have to find a way to keep Nucci off his

back, but it wouldn't be easy. He hadn't thought Nucci would come back to the Green Elephant tonight. Or if he did, that Chip would block him off. But no, the goon had walked right into the back room, just when he was making time with Diane. Buzz was burned up thinking of the way he'd had to turn tail and run, dragging Diane with him.

Nucci was queering his pitch, making him look chicken. But what else could Buzz do? He couldn't stand up to a knife artist like Nucci. What good were your fists when you were up against a shank?

Irrationally his anger turned toward Diane. The stupid little twist! Probably she was getting a big bang out of the whole thing. Man, had she been hot there in the taxi. Her lips had felt like fire and the way she had pressed up against him had really been something. The kid had a lot to learn, but she'd sure found the right guy to teach her the ropes. In spite of his jittery feeling Buzz couldn't help grinning. Give him a month with the babe and he'd have her right where he wanted her, pinned down solid.

The train clanged into the platform and Buzz got aboard, but all the way uptown he couldn't get the memory of Nucci's switchblade out of his mind. He wondered how much Nucci knew about him. He'd learned that Buzz had taken over his old route, but had he guessed that Buzz had put the finger on him for the cops? The idea sent cold shivers along Buzz's spine. Somehow his plans had all gone wrong. He'd thought Nucci would go up the river for a nice long stretch. And here he was back on the streets after less than six months. The zombie must have some real drag.

The subway stop was a block and a half from where

Buzz lived. He felt exposed, naked, as he emerged into the cold glare of the lights. The wind whipped at his light overcoat, chilling his body. He pulled the collar up around his chin and peered up and down the street. No sign of Nucci. But there were plenty of dark alleyways between here and the old brownstone where he lived. Nucci could be waiting in any of them.

Cool it, man, he warned himself; Nucci doesn't know where you're padding down. How could he? But Buzz knew he was whistling in the dark. Nucci had ways of finding things out. And Nucci could have beaten his time easy if he'd taken his cab all the way uptown. Buzz had had to wait ten or twelve minutes on the subway platform.

He'd better not take any chances. He'd walk around the block and come in from the other side. Once he'd made up his mind, he started walking fast. Halfway along the street an old guy stumbled out of an alley and Buzz almost screamed with fear, thinking it was Nucci. A picture flashed in front of his mind of a fight he'd seen between Nucci and an old bum in back of the Green Elephant. Nucci had done a real job on the bum. Slashed him about a dozen times on the face and chest and then stomped all over him. The same thing could happen to Buzz. Here on the empty street nobody was going to help him.

Buzz grew more cautious as he came to the corner of his own block. He slowed down and edged his way along in the shadows of the buildings. He stopped opposite the brownstone where he rented a basement room and sidled into a doorway to look the place over. A naked ten-watt bulb illuminated the basement corridor with a fuzzy light. He saw no one there, but a guy could be waiting in the heavy shadow of the stoop, and you'd never know until you were right on top of him.

Well, that was the chance he had to take. He couldn't hang around all night and if he went peering into every shadow he saw, he'd flip his lid and that was for sure. Anyhow there wasn't one chance in a hundred that Nucci had learned where he was shacking up. Hardly anybody knew. A guy who was really hip never gave out with his address. You made your contacts on the run and if you wanted to meet somebody you passed the word out along the drugstores, the jive joints, the greasy spoons that were the hipster hangouts. That way you always had a place to cat up when the heat was on and nobody the wiser.

He crossed the street in a sprint, so that if Nucci were laying for him he'd have the advantage of the driving impetus of his forward rush. He might as well have taken it easy. There was nothing in the shadow except a crammed trash can. He waited a second, catching his breath, feeling a little sheepish over all his precautions. Just the same, he told himself, better safe than sorry.

The heavy glass door with its rusted wrought-iron grillwork was ajar. As soon as Buzz pushed it open he caught the thick sweet smell of reefer smoke and heard the blatant syncopation of a jazz band. His door at the end of the narrow hall was open. Buzz's jaw tightened with anger. He knew what the score was without going any farther. Hell, just one more thing to be dealt with when he was so worn out that all he wanted was to flop down somewhere and grab himself some kip.

He strode down the hall and stopped in the doorway. It was just the way he'd expected. Dottie Marr was sprawled out on his bed. She'd taken off her shoes and stockings and her sleazy red skirt was rumpled up so that he could see her pale, rounded thighs. One arm hung loosely at her side. The other was propped up on the bedside table. From between her fingers a nearly burned-out reefer let out a wisp of gray smoke.

She hadn't heard him, and while he watched she picked up an empty match flap and bent it backward to form a crutch. She fitted the roach of the reefer into the crutch and took three sharp pokes, drawing the smoke in with a hissing sound, holding it in her lungs, then letting it out slowly. She snubbed out the butt on the ashtray and he saw that it was already loaded with four other roaches. She'd probably been at the tea all night and now she'd be higher than a giraffe's toupee.

She looked up and saw him. She giggled. "Hi, nature boy, I been waitin' for you."

"For God's sakes, how many times I got to tell you, Dottie, if you want to blast in here keep the door shut. The place stinks of the stuff and if some nab comes nosing around he can walk right in."

She giggled again. The sight of her slack face with its smear of carmine for a mouth and the glassy eyes sent a spasm of fury through him. He heeled the door shut and came to her, towering over her.

"Anyway, I told you to keep away from here tonight. I told you to latch on to Wally or go home to your crib. Any place but here."

"What's eating you, Buzz? Couldn't you make time with that uppity little bitch you was haulin' around tonight? Did she get you all worked up and then stand you up? I coulda told you. That's why I been waiting so—"

His hand leapt out, slashing across her face. Then he back-handed her hard against the other cheek. Her head rocked back and a thin line of blood showed where the edge of his ring had sliced into her skin.

She uttered a little choking cry, but she was too stoned to feel the pain or to fight back. She lay staring up at him through glazed eyes, her lips open, breathing hard. He felt his fury mounting higher and higher until it seemed to him that he'd burst. What the hell, he was Buzz Baxter, wasn't he? A smooth cat. A guy who ought to have the world by the tail. Yeah, and what did he rate? A cheap little tart like Dottie Marr.

He stared down at Dottie but he wasn't really seeing her. He was seeing Diane with her cool face and her slender body. She'd be sleeping tonight in that fancy hotel of hers while he was lying in this lousy crib with Dottie beside him. He thought of Frank Nucci stalking him through the dark alley in back of the Green Elephant, and of himself running and running until his lungs nearly burst.

There were other pictures half formed, revolving, disappearing before they could take shape. They were pictures of all the things that had changed a kid named Byron Baktovsky from a scared kid living on the wrong side of the tracks in a grimy New England mill town into Buzz Baxter, the hanger-on about Times Square, the pusher, the piano thumper, the hipster who knew the score and how to find his way around the big town. He saw the tiny two-room apartment where he had lived with his mother after his old man had been killed in a street brawl. He pictured the raid he'd made on a candy store with a couple of other kids and the beating the cops had given him. There were the gray walls of the reformatory where he'd spent more than two years, the cheap honkytonks where he'd played, the two-buck hustlers who'd been his only friends, the garish lights of 42nd Street, the jazz music that ripped at his nerves and set his blood pulsing. There were the five-piece combos of which he'd been a part, the jive parties, the gang bangs. And above everything else there was the nameless, shapeless panic that would never quite let him go but always held him on the edge of flight.

He didn't know how long he'd stood there staring into the past but it was Dottie who brought him around. She was clutching at his hand. "What's the matter with you, Buzz? You act like you was seeing ghosts."

He pulled away from her roughly and started to strip off his clothing. Yeah, he was seeing ghosts, all right. He'd have to let off steam somehow or he'd blow his top for good. The cool air on his naked body made him feel a little better. He switched off the light and sat down on the bed beside Dottie.

His hands passed over her breasts and up to the column of her throat. She giggled a little and he had the sudden impulse to press down hard, to silence her forever.

The idea scared him and helped to clear his head. Hell, he'd have to cut out the weird stuff or he'd turn into a psycho like Nucci. What the hell was the matter with him anyway? He knew what he had to do. Dottie was right here. When it was all over, some of the tension would drain out of him and he could go to sleep.

He drew her to him, feeling her hot breath on his face, her moist, too warm body. He fought down his sudden nausea. What did he have to get himself in an uproar for? This was Dottie. He'd had her plenty of times before, so why get worked up tonight?

He pressed her closer, his hands ripping at her clothing. Get it over quick, he told himself. Then you can grab yourself some sleep. Yeah, a couple of hours of nothingness before it all starts over again.

# 5

The room was gray with the murky light of midafternoon when Buzz woke up. He was twisted to one side, his face to the wall. The long, crooked cracks in the plaster made him think that he was back in the reformatory, and swift panic raced through him. He jerked up with a start. His head was aching and his mouth was dry with the thick taste of stale beer and tobacco. A hard knot formed in the pit of his stomach and made him gag.

He swung his legs over the side of the bed and sat up. He let out his breath with a little whooshing sound as he realized he was in his own pad. Why the hell couldn't he get the memories of the prison out of his mind? That was a long time ago. Now he was a guy who knew the score. Yeah, if his plans went through, pretty soon he'd be in the big time, right up on top. All he had to do was play Diane right. And already he had her eating out of his hand.

He rose unsteadily to his feet and stood swaying a little. Then the door opened and Dottie was in the room. Hell, he'd forgotten all about her. He thought of telling her to broom off, leave him alone. But she had some packages in her arm and he remembered he had only a dime in his pocket. Okay, so she could make him some breakfast, then he'd lay it on the line. He was through with her—for good. Dottie could really screw up his plans for Diane.

He didn't answer when she spoke to him, but sank back on the bed, watching her through slitted eyes as she started to prepare coffee over the electric grill. She really looked crummy, he thought. She'd pinned up a rent in her yellow sweater with safety pins and her red skirt hung unevenly. The whole side of her face was puffed and bruised where he'd hit her last night. What the hell had he ever seen in a quick-trick chippie like Dottie in the first place? He should have given her the bounce long ago.

He remembered the way he'd first seen her. There'd been something fresh and innocent about her then. She'd been a sweet kid dreaming about making the bright lights as an actress. Now the only dreams she ever had were when she got her hands on a strip of bennie. She was peddling herself around the Times Square bars and drugstores. In a year or two she'd be solidly on the hook. Even the reefer circuit wouldn't give her a play. There'd be nothing left for her but the two-bit grinds.

Buzz didn't feel sorry for her. He'd seen too many like her. Besides, he had enough grief of his own. The smell of the coffee made him feel a little better. A cup of java would go good. Maybe it would wash the rank taste out of his mouth and start his brain clicking again.

He got up and put on slacks and a pair of rubber sandals. Dottie handed him a cup of coffee, strong and black the way he liked it. Dottie sat at the table, her legs crossed, watching him. When he was finished she opened up her handbag, took out a reefer and lit it.

"You want a poke, Buzz?"

He'd been trying to ease off the boom, and she knew it. He ought to slap the stick right out of her mouth, but the sweet acrid smoke was tantalizing. What the hell, java wasn't enough to take the edge off when you were really down. What you needed was a little boom so you could start climbing.

He took the reefer from her and sucked in deep. It was sweet gauge, real Mex stuff, and he could feel his nerves untangle and the power seep into him. He took another drag. Already the stuff was beginning to take hold.

Dottie clawed at his hand. "Hey, Buzz, take it easy, will you? That's my last stick."

He relinquished the reefer long enough for her to take a poke, then reached for it again. After that they alternated drags. By the time the stick was burned to a roach, he had little rosy glow. It wouldn't last long. What he needed was some more charge and quick. He had a cache of the stuff hidden away in a crumpled envelope at the bottom of his waste basket, but he didn't want to bring it out—not with Dottie here.

She was bending toward him. "You got a little moolah, Buzz? I could pick up a pack at Riffy's."

"You know I'm stony."

You ain't got nothin' around?"

"No, I ain't got nothin' around. Why don't you see if Riffy will give you a bundle on credit? The creep's eyes pop out every time you show. Why don't you promise him something sweet?"

Her eyes blazed. "Goddamn you, Buzz Baxter. Maybe I will. Maybe I'll—"

He cut her off. "Okay, but don't make a production out of it. You been peddling for a long time. So why not Riffy?"

He expected her to make a scene. Maybe to claw at his face. Then he'd have an excuse to heave her out of his room. He braced himself to grab her quick. After all, he didn't want to be marked up. But all she did was stand there while tears formed in her eyes. Imagine the crazy little twist trying the bawling act on him. He didn't say anything, just waited to see what she'd try next.

She swung away from him and yanked open the door. He could hear her heels clattering in the hallway. He grinned to himself. Maybe this was his lucky day. Maybe he was rid of Dottie for good. He latched the door and crossed quickly to the wastebasket. He scrabbled around in it and came up with the crumpled envelope. He took out a reefer and lit it, staying where he was until the gauge was singing in his blood.

He thought of Diane then. Maybe he ought to call her, fix things up for tonight. But what was the use of dating her unless he had some folding stuff? Tonight, after he made his rounds, he'd have a little moolah to play around with—if Nucci left him alone. He swore under his breath at Nucci, but he didn't have his heart in it. The weed was sending him up on a cloud and everything was rosy and cozy. He giggled a little and caught himself. He settled down in the beat-up armchair and put his feet up on the table. He breathed the smoke in deep and let it out in a spiral. In a little while he'd call up Diane. But right now all he wanted was to take things easy. Anyway he had time on his hands. Yeah, plenty of time.

When he looked at his watch again it was nine-thirty. He could hardly believe it. But that's what boom did to you, made time go all crazy. Okay, so he'd killed the afternoon and most of the evening. That was all to the good. Now he'd better get a hustle on and ankle down to Spasm's place. If he picked up his load of junk by ten, he ought to finish his deliveries and be able to see Diane before midnight.

He got up and started to dress carefully. He didn't believe in wearing sharpie clothes. You dress flashy and the nabs spot you for a punk right away. He always dressed sweet. He chose chocolate-brown slacks, a cotton tweed jacket that looked like a real imported job if you didn't look close, a pearl gray shirt with a button-down collar, and a black knit tie.

His hands were shaking, and he had difficulty knotting the tie. Hell, the gauge was wearing thin already. He dug around for another stick, but he'd used up the lot. He examined the roaches in the ashtray. A couple of them were long enough for a few more drags. He used an empty match flap for a crutch, the way Dottie had the night before. He fitted the roaches into it and dragged deep, holding the stuff as long as he could.

He felt a little better but not much. The rosy glow of the afternoon was gone. All he'd done was slow down the second stage of his reefer jag. Yeah, the bad part was coming now. The anxiety, the fear, the near panic began to claw at him. Pretty soon he'd have the shakes unless he could get a fresh supply of weed.

As soon as he got to Spasm's place, he'd be all right. But then he remembered something that covered his body with cold sweat. Spasm's hotel was the one place where Nucci would know to watch for him. The goon would probably have the place staked off. Yeah, going to Spasm's tonight was like sticking his head in a noose. All the same he had to make a try.

He pulled on his topcoat and tugged his hat low

over, his forehead, to shade his face. Outside the air was still cold and windy. A cab rolled by with its top light on. If he only had the bread he could hail it and be in Times Square in ten minutes. He hesitated at the bus stop on the corner and reached into his pocket—just one measly dime, not enough for bus fare or even the subway. Why hadn't he remembered to borrow a blip from Dottie? Well, it was too late now. He'd have to walk the whole way.

He turned and started downtown, where the bright lights of Times Square filled the sky with a pink glow. It seemed to him that the avenue stretched out for miles and miles and that there were thousands of doorways and alleys where Nucci might be hiding.

The nausea hit him again and he leaned against the side of a building. Tears of self-pity filled his eyes. Here he was a real gone character, a smooth cat, without even enough dough to board a bus. And it was all Diane's fault. If it hadn't been for that crazy taxi ride to her place last night, with Nucci on their tail, he'd be in the clear.

Hatred filled him. He'd bleed Diane plenty for this. Yeah, before he was through with her, he'd pay her off a hundred times over. He took out the dime and flung it into the street. Then with his head down and his shoulders slumped he continued toward Times Square.

## 6

Diane hadn't dared to leave the room all day. Buzz might call and she'd miss him. She had to warn him about the man who had stood in the archway of the church across the street last night, about the threatening telephone call. But more than that, she had to see Buzz.

She moved restlessly about the room, clicking on the radio, snapping it off. Her thoughts were on the events of the preceding night. In her mind she could see the cavorting lights of Times Square, feel the frenetic surging of the crowd around her, hear the whir of traffic, the click and thud of the ski-ball machines in the penny arcades, the screaming jukeboxes, the raucous voices, the vicious ping of rifles in the shooting galleries. The sounds merged into a crazy rhythm with the wail of a saxophone rising shrill and high above the muted contrapuntal beat of Johnnie Lacy's fingers on the piano.

She felt Buzz's lips pressed down on hers and shivered a little. Buzz had been frightened last night, but his fear had added a cogency, a frenzied quality to his kisses. Her mind flicked to the man who had pursued them. The lean powerful body and the gray expressionless face were filled with threat, but there was an undertone of excitement even in the chase. Last night she had been angry with Buzz for deserting her but now all she cared about was being with him again.

She heard the door of her room open and looked up to see the short, dumpy figure of Iris, her mother. Iris's face was devoid of make-up. Her round, soft cheeks looked flabby and her blue eyes watery. Diane turned away from her in sudden distaste. No wonder her father had demanded a divorce from Iris. What man wanted a woman who was all milk and water? With a pang of jealousy she thought of her father, still young and virile-looking, and of his chic second wife. Well,

Willis Griscom knew how to live and so did Diane. After last night she knew she was never going back to the school in Tarymount. She was staying here in New York, close to Buzz. She'd have to tell her mother soon. But she wasn't ready, not yet.

Iris's hand fell lightly on her arm. "You haven't eaten enough to keep a bird alive today, Diane. I'm going to send downstairs for a tray."

"Oh, Mother, please, I'm not hungry."

Iris sighed, "Well, I'll have something sent up anyway. When you see it, maybe you'll change your mind."

Iris went to the phone and asked for room service. Her soft persistent voice went on and on as she discussed the menu. Diane wanted to scream at her, to grab the phone and thrust it back in its cradle. What if Buzz should choose this moment to call and the line was busy?

Diane forced herself to remain quiet. She'd have to have a showdown with Iris in the next few days, but she wanted to be sure of Buzz first. She crossed to the window and looked out over Fifth Avenue. The church was lit up tonight and the inset doorway, where the man had stood, looked peaceful and innocent. Could she have imagined the nameless man standing there watching her window?

Iris lingered on in the room long after the trays had been removed, keeping up a line of small talk to which Diane scarcely listened. Diane wanted to push her out of the room, to be alone in case Buzz should telephone.

The phone shrilled and she snatched it up, keeping her back to her mother.

A voice said, "Is this Miss Diane Griscom?" It wasn't

Buzz, she realized with a sinking feeling. But it wasn't the man who had followed them last night, either. This voice was young, brash, cocky.

"Who are you?"

"Never mind that. I got a message for you—from Buzz. So all I want to know is if you're Diane Griscom."

"Yes. Oh, please—"

"Solid. He says to meet him in the Linwood Drug Store. You know where it is?"

"No."

"It's on Forty-second Street, not far from Eighth Avenue. You come to the corner and look around. You'll spot it easy."

"But why doesn't Buzz call himself? Is anything wrong?"

"Look, lady, I don't know from nothing. This stud comes along and hands me half a buck to give you a tinkle. Okay, so I'm doing like he tells me. He says be here in fifteen or twenty minutes. That's the message. That's all. Period."

The click of the disconnect sounded loud in the room.

Diane laid the instrument down slowly. Why had Buzz paid someone else to make the phone call? Was he running again, fleeing as he had last night from the unknown man? She'd have to get to him quickly. She turned but her mother was blocking her way.

"What is it, Diane?"

"I haven't got time to explain. I've got to go out."

She pushed by her mother and went to the closet. She took out her black coat and pulled the red tam over her blonde hair. But when she started for the foyer her mother was in front of her again. Iris's hand reached for her wrist.

"Diane, I can't let you go. It's too late."

"I tell you there's no time." She tried to draw away but Iris still clung to her. Her breath sucked in with sudden anger.

"Let me go."

"But, Diane—"

Diane's hand lashed out almost of its own volition. She felt the sharp sting of the impact. Her mother backed away and stood looking at her, her mouth open. Red welts sprang up across her cheek.

Diane hesitated. Then she ran for the door. Later on she'd make things up with her mother. Right now she had to find Buzz. She rushed down the stairs and out to the street. A taxi with its dome lighted was cruising along the block. She flagged it down and the brakes squealed as it ground to a stop a few yards in front of her. She raced to it and jumped in.

7

The bracing night air blew the cobwebs out of Buzz's mind. The nearer he got to Times Square the better he felt. This was the hipster's paradise, the one place where he felt at ease. The crowds on the sidewalk were growing thicker. Buzz looked them over. The painted women with their sleazy finery, their faces blue in the flicker of the neon lights. Soldiers on the prowl, stalking dime-store chippies. He held himself more erect, feeling superior to the men and women milling around him. He stopped to look at the blown-up photographs of the hostesses in front of Roseland, and his lips quirked in a smile. That was strictly for the squares, not for a smooth operator like Buzz Baxter.

Pretty soon he'd be right up on top where nobody could touch him. He wondered if Diane realized how much he knew about her father. Willis Griscom was really in the chips, head of a big hotel chain, fronting for the gambling syndicate that had invested money in legitimate businesses so Uncle Sam couldn't put the bite on them for income tax evasion. They were the smart boys—and Buzz would soon be one of them.

He thought of Diane the way he'd first seen her at the hicty frat house up in Tarymount. She'd been standing just a little way from the piano, her lips open, her eyes wide. He'd tabbed her right away for what she was, a crazy kid, heavy with dough, looking for thrills. He'd trailed her out on the balcony and fed her a line and she'd lapped it all up.

He should have tied her up last night, but Nucci had queered his pitch. But maybe Nucci hadn't done him such a bad turn after all. If Diane knew he was in trouble she'd stick to him closer than ever. She'd got a kick out of running through the alley in back of the Green Elephant. Yeah, he could tell by the way she really warmed up to him afterward in the cab.

He was getting close to 42nd Street and he began to move warily. Nucci could step out of the crowd and stick a shank into him before he could even yell. Yeah, putting the finger on Nucci hadn't been such a hot idea, even if it had seemed good at the time. That had been six months ago and there'd been a panic on in the Square. The nabs had been around thick as fleas, picking up everyone who looked suspicious.

Buzz had never been afraid of the fuzz. They'd questioned him a couple of times but he always carried his union card proving he was a musician and had a legitimate reason for being on the turf. Sure, the only jobs he'd had during the last year were with the five-piece combos that toured the college frat houses during the holidays. But nobody needed to know that.

The mob that pushed dope around Times Square had really been hit hard by the panic. The old lags were easy for the cops to spot. The Narcotics Squad had rounded them up in droves. That's when the mob had started recruiting youngsters, cats who knew their way around and how to dress, hipsters like Buzz. He could have cozied into an easy spot if he hadn't tried to outsmart himself. He'd heard from the gang that hung around the Green Elephant that Nucci had a nice route, and it would be all his if Nucci were out of the way.

It had been a pipe fingering Nucci. He'd played it real cool, getting Dottie to tip the nabs with a phony telephone call at just the right moment to put Nucci on ice. How the hell had Nucci got out of the box he was in? It didn't matter, Nucci was free and he must have learned the score. Why else would he be on Buzz's tail? Buzz twisted around to look over the crowd. No sign of Nucci. All the same he'd have to be on his toes to see that the shank-crazy bastard didn't catch up with him.

After he'd got fixed with Diane, he could forget about peddling the junk. Pushers worked for peanuts anyway. He had to laugh every time he read in the paper about some kingpin in the dope racket being busted. Hell, the cops never got beyond the small fry, most of whom scarcely made enough to feed their habits. Sure, the pushers got a chance to handle the folding stuff, but not for long. You had to pay off all along the way—waiters, bellboys, hotel clerks, somebody wherever you made the score. You were lucky if you ended up the night with a dime note for yourself—and for that you took big chances. Every time Buzz thought of the sentences handed out to pushers he broke into a cold sweat. Ten, maybe fifteen years. It was a long stretch, even if you did it on both ears.

Up ahead Buzz could see the fleabag joint where Spasm lived, a dive called the Bassett Arms. He walked along the other side of the street, keeping an eye cocked for Nucci. He passed the place twice but if Nucci was hanging around, he'd really buried himself deep.

He crossed the street and entered the Bassett Arms. There was a crummy hallway with yellowing tiles that were imbedded in dirt. The whole place stank of soiled bedding and unclean bodies. The hallway led back to an alcove where a reception desk was set. The fat punk behind the counter gave him a nod. Buzz reflected he'd have to give him a five-spot when he came back from his rounds. There'd be a buck for the elevator boy too. Yeah, everybody and his brother had his hand out.

Buzz took the cage up to the top floor and slammed down the hall to Spasm's room. He thumbed the bell, giving the signal, a long ring and then two short ones. What the hell, why play games like this? Spasm would know he was on his way up. The jerk of a desk clerk would have seen to that. Still, maybe Spasm was right. It was always best to cover yourself double.

The door swung open a few inches then jolted against a rusted chain. Through the crack, Buzz could see Spasm in his wheelchair. In the dim hallway, the little spastic's face seemed gray and featureless. The light from the corridor made opaque moons out of his thick glasses.

Spasm didn't let him in; Spasm never admitted anyone to his room if he could help it. The spastic was a smart cookie. The door looked flimsy but it was made of sheet metal and it would take a bulldozer to break the chain. Whenever the cops forced their way in, Spasm always dummied up. So what the hell could they do to him? You couldn't beat up a guy in a wheelchair. Especially when he was throwing fits all over the place.

Yeah, Spasm was a valuable man to the syndicate. Their runners brought him the junk in big lots and he parceled it out to the pushers. There was one iron-bound rule. You paid off Spasm the same night you got your load, after you made your rounds. If you didn't there was trouble, real trouble. The syndicate's goons saw to that.

Spasm looked him over through the crack without saying anything. Then he wheeled his chair away. He was back in a minute or so with a bundle in his hand but he didn't pass it to Buzz right away. Instead he said in his high, cracked voice, "Hey, Buzz, you know Nucci got sprung?"

Buzz tried to play it tough. "So what?"

The spastic's thin body twitched. "So nothing, if you think you can handle him. Orders is Nucci's to get no more stuff. The nabs are wise to him. But get this straight, Buzz. We ain't giving you no protection from Nucci. You're on your own."

Buzz felt a cold finger run along his spine. He'd thought maybe if he talked to Spasm, the big boys would pull Nucci off his back. Now, there was nothing to do but bluff it out. "I'm not scared of the crazy goon."

Spasm gave a twittering laugh that made Buzz want

to poke him. The door slammed shut and Buzz was alone in the hall.

He turned around slowly. The backs of his hands were moist with sweat and he had a funny feeling in the pit of his stomach. He always felt this way when he'd just picked up his load from Spasm, but tonight it was worse than ever. Nucci could be lurking on the steps or in one of the dim corridors. Or maybe he'd tipped the nabs off and they'd grab him as soon as he left the hotel.

The elevator seemed a long way off. And if Nucci were hiding some place close at hand, waiting to pounce on him, he'd have Buzz penned in a squeeze. Better to take the stairs. Buzz moved gingerly to the landing. He'd gone down just two or three steps when he heard a slithering sound up above. He pressed up against the wall, barely managing to stifle a cry.

Someone had moved to the balustrade and was looking down. Buzz couldn't see anything but a blurred shadow. He braced himself, wondering what to do next. He started creeping down the steps one by one, but he hadn't gone far when his nerve broke and he clattered and banged down the rest of the flight.

At the bottom he almost fell. He twisted around and looked upward. A woman stared back at him. He could make out the frizzled yellow hair, the smeared lipstick, the big patches of rouge on her cheeks. She was wearing a soiled housecoat with a design of huge roses. She clutched it around her throat. Buzz caught her number right away, a cheap two-buck chippie trying to hustle herself up a john for the night. And she'd nearly made him flip his lid.

He wasn't scared any longer. He was sore. What he ought to do was go back up there and bash her teeth in for the scare she'd thrown into him. Yeah, he ought to slam her around good. But that wasn't playing it smart, not with all the junk he had on him. Besides he didn't want to go up the stairs again. For all he knew the old bag might be working as a decoy for Nucci.

He clung to the railing and all of a sudden he wanted to bawl. At first he didn't know what was the matter with him. Then he remembered how long it had been since he'd had his last stick. He started down the stairs again, no longer caring about the clatter of his shoes on the worn marble steps.

8

Diane had expected Linwood's to be one of the big, garishly lit drugstores which dot the Times Square area. Instead it was long, narrow and dingy, with a littered counter running the length of one side. She stopped by the racks of paper-covered books and looked for Buzz. He was nowhere in sight. A group of teenagers, dressed identically in tight fitting jeans, black windbreakers and paratroop boots gave her the eye and one of them let out a wolf whistle. She walked on past them and took a stool near the end of the counter. She glanced at her watch. Not quite fifteen minutes since she'd got the call. Probably Buzz wasn't expecting her so soon.

The white-jacketed youth in attendance was sweet-talking a fat woman whose gross body seemed to ooze over the white plastic counter. The woman turned and looked at her with unblinking eyes. She tucked up a stray wisp of her hennaed hair. "What's a cute little doll like you doing in a crummy joint like this?"

Diane didn't answer. The soda jerk moved toward her, his mouth opened in a grin. There was a swagger to his chunky body. "What'll it be, miss?"

The cocky voice was familiar. It was he who had telephoned her at the hotel. She hesitated and he raised an eyebrow quizzically. "Say, your name wouldn't be Diane, would it?"

"Yes. Where's Buzz? Why did he hire you to call for him?"

"Look, baby. I don't even know which end is up. In my racket you learn to keep your nose clean. That way you stay healthy."

"Tell me where to find him."

"Okay, sister, don't get in an uproar. This stud slipped me another four bits to give you a message. But I don't like the way this guy's been pulling the creep act. I been thinking maybe I should tell him to shove it. What's this guy to you? You on the junk?"

"Never mind about that. Just tell me what he said."

The boy shrugged. "Okay, I ain't your uncle. He's downstairs in one of the telephone booths. The last one in the line."

She didn't wait to hear more. At the back of the store she could see the big sign that read *Telephones* and the red arrow pointing downward. She slipped off the stool and hurried to the stairway.

At the foot of the stairs the booths stretched out in a narrow line. Three ceiling lights should have lit up the concrete passageway, but two of them were out. The booth at the end was closed, but a light shone through the glass panel. Diane had a swift premonition of danger. Not for herself but for Buzz. Why was he so afraid?

She moved swiftly along the dim passage, not daring to call Buzz's name. A sleeve of a gray coat was visible in the lighted booth. She caught a glimpse of movement and the door swung open, leaving the booth in darkness. The man was on her before she realized that he wasn't Buzz. One hand circled her waist and the other clapped over her mouth.

She tried to bite the man's palm but the skin was tough as leather. He clamped down harder until her jaw throbbed with pain. She looked up into his face, the pale slate-gray eyes, the colorless lips curled back in a grimace.

He said, "I knew you'd come. You really got hot pants over Buzzy boy, ain't you? I don't get it. How's a punk like Baxter rate a sweet piece of goods like you? Why don't you wise up and pick yourself a man?"

Diane remained still, too terrified to struggle. The man jerked her close to him, so that she could feel his hard, angular body. His voice was at once threatening and ingratiating. "You hung up on me last night, sister. That wasn't nice, not nice at all. This time you're going to hear me out, if you know what's good for you."

She tried to pull away, but his arm was like coiled metal. "I ain't asking much. Nothing that you wouldn't give Buzz. All I want's a good time, and everything'll be solid between me and Buzz. I'll let bygones be bygones. Buzz can even keep my old route. So you just play along and everything will be george."

She twisted in his grasp and kicked out at him. He didn't even seem to notice. "I ain't in no hurry. You talk things over with Buzz. Maybe he'll see it my way."

There were shuffling, uncertain footsteps on the stairs. The man looked up and his voice changed to a hoarse whisper. "Right now I'm letting you go, sister.

But don't put up no squawk. It wouldn't be healthy. Not for you. Not for Buzz. And there's a little gadget I want to show you before you go."

His hand dropped from her mouth, dipped into his pocket. Something flat, metallic, lay in his palm. His thumb triggered it and a six-inch blade snaked out. The feeble light caught the honed steel and gave it a silver brightness.

The man laughed. "That's for Buzz, sweetheart. Unless you come across. You tell that to Buzzie boy. Tell him there's just one way to get Frank Nucci off his back."

The footsteps on the stairs had stopped. Diane broke free and spun around. The fat woman with the hennaed hair stood on the bottom step. She was grasping the railing with both hands and peering near-sightedly along the gloomy passage.

"What goes on?" she asked drunkenly. "You two smooching or having a fight? Tell Nellie about it."

Diane ran toward her. The fat woman put out a beefy arm as though to embrace her. "Whatsa matter, girlie? Has this guy been getting fresh? Nellie'll fix him. Nellie knows the score."

Diane pushed on past her, feeling the woman's bulging body, soft and warm beneath the sleazy dress, smelling the gin-laden breath. She ran up the rest of the flight. There was no sound of pursuit behind her. She kept on running, through the store, out on to 42nd Street. Instinctively she turned toward Times Square.

The cavorting lights loomed up in front of her. The huge blinking signs that advertised soft drinks, Kleenex and dog food. She slowed up, threading her way through the crowds until a hand grasped her elbow. She stared into the face of a young soldier.

"Hi, beautiful. What's the rush?"

She shook herself free but he stayed by her side. "Don't be that way, beautiful. I won't bite you."

Across the street she saw the red and green bulbs that spelled out Pleasure Palace in gigantic letters. That was the shooting gallery where she'd met Buzz the night before. He might be there now. She darted out into the traffic. Brakes screamed and a horn blasted as a taxi swerved to miss her. The back fender whipped at her skirt. She glimpsed the driver's face, distorted with anger. He bellowed at her, but the words were lost in the pandemonium of sound that filled the street.

The doors of the Pleasure Palace were wide open. She pushed in. The place was jammed. Even if Buzz were here, she'd never find him. A group of loungers in sharpie clothes called out to her in staccato Spanish. She ignored them. At the far end of the room she thought she caught a glimpse of Buzz, leaning against one of the Pokerino machines. She cried his name and hurried toward him. A man's figure blocked her way. A voice, soft and wheedling, spoke to her. She saw the tan coat, the too-sharp crease of the chocolate-colored trousers, the pointed two-toned shoes. She didn't look up but circled around him.

A wave of disappointment broke over her. There was no one by the Pokerino machine now. She looked about in desperation. No sign of Buzz. Maybe she had been mistaken. Maybe she had wanted too much to believe that he was here. There was no place for him to have gone except down the miniature stairway that led to a sideshow and flea circus. She couldn't imagine Buzz going to a flea circus.

The noises confused her. The rapid ping-ping-ping

of the rifles, a barker shouting his spiel over a microphone, the shuffle of the ski-ball games, the raucous voices. She had to find Buzz, warn him about Nucci. But she couldn't think clearly.

The Green Elephant. Why hadn't she thought of the Green Elephant in the first place? It wasn't far. Someone there would be able to tell her how to find Buzz—Johnnie Lacy, Chip, the girl with the red skirt. She took a step toward the door. The young soldier whom she'd thought she'd shaken was waiting for her.

"Hi, there, baby. Tried to give me the brush-off, didn't you?"

"Leave me alone."

Something about her tone made him give ground. She brushed by him and was back in the milling crowd. Tonight 42nd Street seemed a neon jungle. The concrete sidewalk was like rubber foam, sucking at her feet, holding her away from Buzz.

Eighth Avenue was darker. She was glad to be free of the glaring lights, the jumble of sound. She walked with her head down, glancing up only to search for the flickering neon of the Green Elephant. She saw it up ahead and hurried a little faster.

She climbed the crooked steps and opened the door to the dim, smoke-filled room. It was crowded, as it had been the night before. Voices slurred with drink screamed over the pulsating rhythm of Johnnie Lacy's band. She took a step or two and then Chip was blocking her path. His blue-jowled face and heady eyes held hostility. There was an implacable set to the thick body encased in the shabby blue tuxedo.

She asked quickly, "Is Buzz here?"

"Naw." Chip's head wagged slowly from side to side. "He was around a while ago but he went."

"Where? Tell me where."

"How should I know? I ain't his brother."

"When did he leave?"

"Look, miss, I ain't got time to check on alla the studs who ankle in here. We don't have no time clock." He laughed at his own joke.

Diane tried to sidle past him but he still blocked her. "Let me talk to Johnnie Lacy."

"No can do. Unaccompanied dames ain't allowed here."

"But I've got to find Buzz."

Chip's voice kept its harsh monotone, but there was a hint of threat behind it. "We don't make the rules, miss. We let you in here and maybe the cops lift our license. So be nice and take a walk, huh?"

She tried to move forward again but her shoulder struck against his chest, and he forced her back. "I told you Buzz ain't here and he don't pass out the word where he cats up. Now beat it, girlie, because there's fuzz around. We don't want no trouble here."

She thought of throwing herself against him, clawing his face, making a scene. But it wouldn't do any good. It would only make it harder for her to find Buzz. And the man's body seemed massive, capable of crushing her.

There was nothing to do but turn away, back down the two stone steps to Eighth Avenue. She stood uncertainly in the shadows, tears stinging her eyes. What next? If she returned to the hotel, she'd have to face her mother, start explaining things. She couldn't stand that tonight. Not without seeing Buzz. Her mouth set in a stubborn line. She wouldn't be beaten so easily. Somehow she'd get into the Green Elephant. If all she needed was a man to accompany her, she'd pick one up. It should be easy. The young soldier who'd followed her must be somewhere about. She thought of his pink, flushed face. He wouldn't be hard to handle. Once she got the information she wanted from Johnnie Lacy, she'd be able to rid herself of the soldier.

She set out rapidly along the dark street. She'd go back to the Pleasure Palace. Then a new thought struck her. She'd have to pass Linwood's again. A thread of fear plucked at her nerves. Nucci might still be lurking there. He might force himself on her again. Maybe he was following her now, waiting for her to lead him to Buzz. She tried to assure herself she'd be safe on 42nd Street. But would she be? If Nucci tracked her down, who among the derelicts, the drunks, the youngsters out for a spree, would help her? Nucci's gray face seemed to rise in front of her and she gave an involuntary shudder.

Footsteps pounded on the sidewalk behind her, slapping on the cement with a hard, rhythmic beat. A harsh voice called out for her to wait. She turned, half-crouching, ready to run, her fear of Nucci mounting to panic.

A figure rushed toward her. In the darkness she couldn't recognize who it was, but it wasn't Nucci.

The man stopped, spraddle-legged, in front of her. "For God's sake, Diane, cool it. What's the matter with you?"

The stubby body, the broad pale face, the horn-rimmed glasses, the kinky reddish hair were all familiar, but in her confusion she couldn't place him.

He was breathing heavily. "I didn't mean to scare ya. Don't you know me? I'm Wally Jones."

She gave a little laugh.

Wally was talking fast. "Johnnie Lacy saw Chip

giving you the bum's rush and as soon as there was a break, he told me to hustle out and find you. For Pete's sake, what's a dame like you doing all alone in a jive dive like the Elephant? Where's Buzz, anyhow?"

"That was what I was trying to learn. I've got to find him, Wally. You'll help me, won't you?"

"Sure, sure. But that's no easy order. Buzz is a cat who hops around plenty. What's more he don't like nobody sniffing around his business. It won't be no cinch to pin him down."

"I don't care. I've got to warn him. A man named Nucci's after him, threatening to knife him."

"That ain't no news for Buzz. Why do you think he pulled a creep out of the Elephant last night?"

"But Nucci phoned me. And then tonight—" she hesitated, not wanting to tell the whole story. "He told me unless—"

Wally's face grew grim. "You don't need to draw me no pictures, Diane. I know Nucci. He's a real weirdie. There's two things he goes for in a big way, girls and that shank of his."

"Then he means it about cutting up Buzz."

"He means it, all right. I hate to tell you this but you're playing with something more dangerous than dynamite. Nucci's one wrong guy. Steer clear of him."

"But Buzz has got to know."

"Look, Diane, maybe I'm sticking my neck out, but I'll try to sniff Buzz out and tell him the score. You leave it to me and go home and grab yourself some kip."

"Kip?"

"Shut-eye—sleep. That's what you need."

"No, Wally. I'm going along with you."

"You don't understand. I'll be hitting some rough

spots."

"I don't care."

"Johnnie wouldn't like it. Johnnie said to make sure you was okay."

"Who cares what Johnnie says? Either I'm going with you or I'm hunting for Buzz on my own."

Wally looked at her for a moment uncertainly, then his face cracked into a grin.

"Okay, Diane, I guess you win. Let's dangle."

## 9

Buzz was feeling rosy again. Way up on top looking down. The sidewalk beneath his feet was fleece-lined, smooth as velvet. The buildings stood out sharp and clear. As soon as he'd made his first sale of the junk that Spasm had handed him, he'd cut into a shop where the stud behind the counter sold weed. He'd bought himself a load of bombers, done up real neat to look like regular cigarettes. You could take your drags right out on the street and nobody the wiser unless they got close enough to sniff the stuff.

Yeah, he was really soaring, without a care in the world. Peddling junk was safe enough if you knew the ropes. And Buzz was plenty sharp. Soon after he'd taken over Nucci's route, he'd shifted all the scoring points. Not that he'd been afraid of Nucci then. He'd thought the creep would be in the slammer for years to come. It was just a matter of taking precautions. He'd seen too many pushers get picked up because they got careless.

Buzz was a cat who didn't believe in taking chances. You made yourself a set of rules and stuck by them.

Rule number one was never to make a sale where a third person could see you. You never knew who might be a Fed. The Feds were smart, really on their toes. Agents had disguised themselves as countermen, bus boys, ushers in the movie houses where the junkies were known to congregate. Buzz liked to score behind a locked door whenever he could. His favorite spot was in the cubicle of a washroom. Nobody could get in to you without warning, and when you left you had plenty of opportunity to case the room. If you saw anything suspicious, you could dump the load and flush it down the drain. Unless you were busted with the stuff on you, the nabs couldn't build up a case that would stand up in court.

One good thing about pushing horse was you never had to pressure your customers. They were always where you told them to be, right on the dot. They'd be clawing you for the stuff, so eager to get it that they hardly put up a squawk when the price tripled. And a cat who was on the hook would have the dough on hand, too. Somehow he'd get it, no matter what chances he had to take. Buzz had seen junkies pull muggings and rollings right in Times Square when they had monkeys on their backs.

Sometimes Buzz was tempted to try the white stuff himself. Lately the reefers hadn't been sending him the way they used to. The hipsters said that heroin gave you ten times the bang that the grass did. Maybe it would be worth a try; a guy as hip as Buzz would never get hooked. Just when Buzz had about made up his mind, he'd spot some hophead with the screaming meemies. The uncontrollable yawning, the tears streaming down their eyes, the twitching of the facial muscles, the way they bent over with the cramps, all gave him the shivers. No, he didn't want any. And the safest way not to get caught was never to take the first shot. All the same . . .

Buzz broke off his thoughts. He'd have to keep his mind on business until he completed his rounds. He'd got a scare earlier in the night. He'd been ready to pull a score in the Pleasure Palace. He'd worked out the method himself. He and the junkie would squeeze into one of the automatic photography booths, the kind where you put a quarter in the slot and got your picture taken. There was a curtain on each booth and when it was pulled nobody could see you handing out the junk or pocketing the folding stuff. But just as he'd made sure the coast was clear, he'd seen Diane at the entrance of the Pleasure Palace. He'd been ready to flip. He'd liked to have knocked her ears down for chasing around after him. The crazy little trim would have to be taught a lesson, but there'd be time for that later. Meanwhile he couldn't afford a scene, especially in the Pleasure Palace. So he'd ducked down the stairs to the flea circus. That was really a laugh, watching the big bald-headed guy pull his stuff for the ginkos.

Buzz had only one more call; then he'd be through. But this one he didn't like. Not that Gladys Maintree wasn't okay. As a matter of fact, he always got a bang out of going to her place. She was a dame whom you couldn't tell to meet you in any of the fleabag joints where he hung out. Even in a drugstore or café, she'd stand out like a tramp in the lobby of the Waldorf.

When Buzz had first hit the town, Maintree had been right up on top. She'd had her name in lights over the marquee of the Museum Theater and her pictures in the Sunday supplements. She'd hit the gossip columns as often as Bankhead or Cornell. Yeah, she'd reached for the moon and grabbed it. But she hadn't held it for long. She'd hit the skids and slid right down into the cellar. Not many people knew why, but Buzz was one who did. She was praying to the white god. Buzz was supplying her with the stuff.

Maintree had put on a lot of poundage, especially around the hips, and her neck and arms were flabby. Even so, when she put on her war paint she still had what it takes. Any cat who saw her would do a double take and there were plenty who would recognize her. That was why Buzz took the stuff directly to her place, just the way Nucci had done.

That was the rub. Nucci would know he'd be calling on Maintree some time tonight. Maintree lived in an apartment on Fifth, facing the park. There were plenty of places for Nucci to hide without anybody being the wiser. He could watch Buzz go in and be right on top of him when he came out again. Buzz thought of Nucci's switchblade and shivered. Maybe he ought to give Maintree the go-by, but if he did she'd complain to Spasm. And if Spasm ever got the idea that Buzz was chicken, that he'd deuced out because of Nucci, then Buzz'd be out on his ear.

He didn't have far to go now. Maintree's apartment house was near the end of the block. He slowed his pace, scanning the street and the park for signs of Nucci. The block was empty of pedestrians, but there was still plenty of traffic. The headlights of the cars made shadows jump all over the place. He couldn't see Nucci, but that didn't mean a thing. The creep could be in a doorway, in the entry between two buildings, behind the shrubbery.

The best thing was to move fast. The doorman was

off duty. Buzz pulled at the heavy glass door and entered the brightly lit foyer. He felt better as soon as he was inside with the door between him and the street. The desk clerk looked up and then away again. Buzz had slipped him a fin every now and then. The elevator door was open and the Puerto Rican kid, Luis, was sitting on a stool in front of it. Luis was wise, a kid who knew the score. He followed Buzz into the car and shut the door, then just stood there waiting. Buzz would have liked to have kicked him, right where it would hurt most. But Luis had him by the short hairs. If Buzz didn't play, Luis could tip off the nabs.

Buzz dug out a couple of singles and tucked them in Luis's hip pocket. The car shot up as though it were automatic. It stopped on the sixteenth floor and the door slid open. Buzz didn't look at Luis but started down the carpeted hallway. Maybe if things went right with Diane he'd be living in a joint like this himself pretty soon and then he wouldn't have to take any crap off of crumbs like Luis either.

Maintree must have been on the lookout for him. She was at the door almost as soon as his thumb touched the bell. Buzz shoved by, then turned to face her. She was in a rose-colored hostess gown that fell low over her full breasts. Her dark hair hung loose around her shoulders and her face was devoid of make-up. Even so she looked good, Buzz thought. But she wasn't giving him any time to study her. Her fingers were like claws on his arm.

She said, "My God, Buzz, I thought you were never coming. I'm dying. In another hour, the monkey'd be crawling all over me. Come on, give me the stuff."

Buzz snapped his fingers and grinned at her. "The

moolah first, sweetheart."

"Oh, for God's sake, did I ever pull anything on you?"

Buzz still grinned. "I gotta collect first. You know that."

"Okay. Okay." She went into the next room, leaving the door open behind her. Buzz watched as she crossed to the dresser. In the polished surface of the mirror he could see her reflected figure. She reached for an alligator-skin bag, her hands fumbling awkwardly at the gold clasp. With shaking fingers she extracted a roll of bills, letting some of them spill across the top of the dresser. Buzz whistled to himself. This dame was really heavy with dough, loaded down with it.

She thrust the bills back into the bag hurriedly. Buzz turned away, strolled toward the window so that she wouldn't catch wise to what he'd seen. He needn't have bothered. All she had on her mind was the horse. She was breathing hard and her eyes were hot and moist when she came back to him.

She handed him a double sawbuck. "Come on, give it to me, Buzz. I tell you I'm dying."

Once she had the envelope in her hand she forgot all about him. There was a candle burning in a decorated brass brazier. She went to it and started cooking up a cap. She had a professional kit, a real glossy setup, not the spoon with a bent handle and the eye dropper and needle of the Times Square junkie. Just the same she was goofing her shot, her fingers trembling, spilling the stuff in her eagerness.

He looked away and moved closer to the window. From here he could see the park and the street below. The crawling taxis were like toys and the occasional pedestrians seemed to be drawn along on puppet strings. Was Nucci waiting down there in the shadow of one of the trees? A flicker of light drew his attention. Someone standing behind a parked car had lit a cigarette. Buzz stared at the miniature figure. Nucci? How could he tell? All he could see from here was a gray hat, merging into a dark coat. But even so, there was something implacable, enduringly patient about the waiting man.

Buzz pressed closer to the window. He could feel the weakness in his knees and the quivering sensation that passed through his body like tiny tendrils of flame. Damn Nucci! Why did the creep scare him so? But he knew the answer. It was the knife. Ever since his days in the reformatory, a shank had given him the shakes. There had always been some tough guy in stir who ruled the roost with a knife.

Now it was the same thing with Nucci. The stud down below didn't move. Buzz's conviction that it was Nucci mounted until it was certainty. A voice just beside him made him jump. He hadn't heard Gladys Maintree cross the room. Her eyes had grown small and the tense white look had disappeared, leaving her face calm, almost as though she were in a trance. Her voice had smoothed out too, lost its thin, reedy quality and taken on rich undertones.

"What's the matter, Buzz? You look as if you were seeing ghosts. You got something on your mind?"

He managed a lopsided grin. "You always got worries in my business."

"What you need is a taste of your own medicine."

"Uh-uh. I'll settle for a reefer."

She laughed lightly. "Kid stuff. You don't know what living is until you've tried the white."

He didn't reply but he reached for her. His hand, cupped beneath the fabric of the loose housecoat, rested on the warm flesh of her breast. She didn't move away or respond. Her face was grave, statue-like, and her lidded eyes without expression. He kissed her. Her lips were warm and yielding but they did not move beneath his.

She took a step back from him and he let her go. She said, "I'm high already but that's not enough. I want to fly tonight, really soar.'

A sudden spurt of anger flared within him. He wasn't a man to her, just part of a junkie dream. He'd like to grab her, rip the housecoat off her. But that wasn't playing it smart. She wasn't ready yet, wouldn't be until she'd had another shot. She wouldn't let anything get in the way of that. If he tried any rough stuff, she might scream, make a scene, get him tossed out. Maybe right into Nucci's waiting arms.

He forced himself to cool down and watched her as she went back to the brazier. She picked up the candle and the kit and carried them into the bedroom. He lit a bomber and dragged deep of the sweet smoke. He waited until his nerves were steady before he followed her into the room.

He sat down on the edge of the bed watching the almost ritualistic movement of her hands. The trembling had gone from her fingers and they performed with a smooth, expert skill. Her face was calm, made soft by the shadowy light of the flickering candle.

When she had finished, she came to him, stood beside him. She unfastened the housecoat, let it drop around her ankles. He sucked in his breath with sudden desire. He reached upward, pulled her naked body to him. She fell across him, sprawling on the bed. He kissed her throat but she didn't move. Her eyes were open but filmed over, sightless.

As swiftly as his desire had sprung up, it went away. He pushed her aside and stood up, swearing softly. She lay motionless. He leaned over and struck her hard with the flat of his hand. Her lips parted in a little moan, and that was all.

An uneasy fear swept over him and he began to shake. He ought to get out of here. He had a vision of the carpeted hallway and of himself racing madly along the echoing corridor. Beyond lay the streets, the dim gray streets, with Frank Nucci lying in wait behind every parked car.

"Cut it out, man. For God's sake cool it." The sound of his own voice startled him at first, then steadied him. What the hell had got into him, flipping his lid like that? What he needed was a little boom to straighten himself out.

He lit up and hissed in the smoke in short deep puffs until the roach scorched his fingers. He was still sweating, but he was steady. Okay, he told himself, let's take a look at the score. The Maintree dame got stoned. So what? You've seen it happen plenty of times before. So why did it get through to you? Because you got the wind up over Nucci and she was standing between you and that crazy bastard's knife. All right, all right, you still got a safe place to stay, and in the morning when you've cooled off, you'll find a way to put it over on Nucci. You're a hell of a lot smarter than he is, aren't you? All you need is a little time.

He was feeling good again. Geez, all you had to do in this life was use your head and you could always get in the clear.

He went to the dresser and opened the alligator bag. The bills were there, all squashed up in the bottom.

He took them out and thrust them into his pocket without even bothering to count them.

Then he went back to the bed where Gladys Maintree was lying.

## 10

The door was bright red, with an ornamental knocker in the form of a gilded dragon. From somewhere behind it rose the thin, monotonous wail of a Chinese lute. Diane leaned against the cracked, grimy wall and looked back over the three flights of high, narrow stairs she had just climbed. She was exhausted, but underneath her weariness lay an undertone of excitement. Her search for Buzz had almost lost its meaning and become an object in itself.

Her eyes flicked to Wally Jones, who stood facing her. Wally's face was pale and drawn, with a prickling of sweat across his forehead. He said, "This is the end of the line, Diane. If we don't flush Buzz this time we might as well call it quits. Anyway, Buzz has probably folded up for the night and gone to his pad."

Diane didn't answer. Ever since she had met Wally, they'd been on the move. There had been scores of strange doors, endless stairways. Some of the doors had led to dingy cellar clubs where teenage couples, their bodies plastered to each other, scarcely moved as they undulated to the rock 'n' roll music that slammed out of a radio or recorder. Other doors had admitted them to the sleezy, raucous cabarets of Little Spain resounding with the harsh frenetic jungle beat of Afro-Cuban music. Still others led to fag joints, to shabby bars with five-piece combos or stepped-up jukeboxes, to drugstores where Wally whispered a word or two to the counterman, to crowded garish hotel rooms where young girls slid in and out of the embraces of older men and where the air was stifling with the stench of marijuana, to shooting parlors where shadowy figures remained motionless listening to muted music.

They hadn't found Buzz. But several times they'd been told that he'd been around earlier. In each place Wally left a message for Buzz in case he showed, that they'd round up the night in Starr's Restaurant.

This was an alien world to Diane. A world where shadow and movement and glaring light blended together to form a backdrop against which figures moved, now furtively, now with abandon, the hunter and the hunted, the bold, the frightened, the lost, all on an endless quest that was the reflection of her own search for Buzz. This was Buzz's world and its stark reality, its intensity of feeling, its shabbiness and its glitter, its constantly shifting movement, beat out a strange rhythmic pattern in which the blare of the saxophone, the steady climbing wail of the horn, the boogie beat of the off-tone piano played in a cellar club were counterpointed by the shuffle and drag of feet on concrete, the mounting scream of a police siren, the coarse laughter, the voices high-pitched or growling, the swirl of traffic and the almost inaudible, yet ever present tattoo of threat, warning, fear and danger.

She drew her mind back to the red Chinese door and to Wally. He was saying, "This is another swish joint. Maybe we ought to give it a miss."

Diane shook her head. "Not if there's a chance of Buzz's being here."

Wally lifted a shoulder in resignation. "Just as you say." He raised the knocker and let it fall. A peephole just above the dragon slid open and an eye examined them. Then the door swung back. The man standing in front of them was short and roly-poly, his obese body swathed in a Chinese robe embroidered with a dragon. His skin was pale and his blue eyes watery. His lips were too red, pursed into the shape of a rosebud. He spoke in a high, piping voice. "Oh, Wally, it's so wonderful to see you. Why haven't you come before?"

"Can it; you know I'm straight."

"Now, Wally—"

"Climb off it," Wally said gruffly. "I'm looking for Buzz."

"Buzz is such a divine boy, but the prices he's charging. Wally, you must speak to him."

Wally's hand shot out and he caught the loose folds of the kimono in his fist. "Cut the fruit cake. All I want to know is if Buzz is here."

"Now, Wally, don't be rough."

"Goddamn it. Tell me."

"No. He was here a long time ago. He wouldn't stay. I asked him to stay."

Wally gave a push that sent the man reeling back into the room, then he kicked the door shut. He swung around to Diane, his lips tight. He said, "Okay, this is where we came in—no Buzz. What next? Shall I take you home or to Starr's?"

Diane gave a little laugh. "It will have to be Starr's. Maybe Buzz will be waiting."

For a moment Wally's jaw set in an obstinate line. "Look, Diane, you don't owe this stud nothing. How many times do I have to tell you, Buzz is a guy who can ice his own cake?"

Diane placed her fingers on his wrist. Wally sighed but he managed a feeble grin. He spread his hands in a mocking gesture. "What's the use of talking to a dame who's holding a torch?"

Starr's was an all-night cafeteria with bright overhead lights that made the white tiles glitter. The glass display cases caught the gleam too. As they pushed in through the revolving door Diane saw that the hands of the big wall clock pointed to a few minutes of four. The place was almost empty, but by the time they had gotten their trays, it had begun to fill up. Starr's was the gathering place for those who worked the night beat around Times Square—the bandsmen, the concessionaires, the entertainers, even the waiters and the hat-check girls who knocked off work at four. They came thronging in, laughing, jostling one another, their loud conversation spiced with jive talk.

Diane followed Wally to a table close to the huge plate glass window that faced 42nd Street. The crowd on the street had thinned out and the neon lights seemed to blink tiredly in the murky darkness.

She took a sip of the scalding black coffee and looked across the table at Wally. He peered back at her, his eyes enormous behind the thick-lensed glasses.

She asked, "Do you think he'll come?"

"How should I know? Somewhere along the line, someone must have told him we'd be waiting."

"Could Nucci have—" She cut off the words. Wally stirred and when he spoke, his voice was edged with anger. "Let's quit messing around and talk turkey. Why don't you give Buzz the kiss-off? Why don't you go back where you belong?"

Her eyes met his. "Where's that, Wally? Where is it

I belong? In a girl's finishing school? In some backwater town where I'll be protected from life, where I'll never know what's going on until it's too late?"

"Cut it out, Diane. You weren't wearing blinkers tonight. You saw the dives where Buzz hangs out. How do you think Buzz earns his jack?"

Diane looked away. She knew all right, even though until now she'd been unwilling to admit the truth, even to herself. Buzz was a pusher. It had to be that way. But why? Buzz had a wild, fierce magic in his fingers. He should be with a top-name band.

Wally's voice went on inexorably. "I'm sticking my neck out a mile. But there's some things I gotta say. Why should a sweet kid like you be wearing out your ankles for a bum like Buzz?"

Diane's eyes flashed with sudden anger. "If you feel that way, why have you been helping me to find Buzz?"

"Let's clear the line. Buzz don't shine for me. In my books he's a two-timing louse."

"Then why?"

"Because Johnnie Lacy told me to stick to you. And Johnnie's a down cat, the real goods."

Diane's mind swung to Johnnie Lacy, remembering the lean, compact body, the dark face with its hollowed cheeks, the black almost fanatical eyes. "I don't understand. Why should Johnnie care what happens to me?"

"I don't know, Diane. It looks like he's got a thing about you. Johnnie's a hard cat to dig, but he's solid. Really solid. He ain't another hipster on the make. He's a guy who's dedicated to jazz, a guy who cares enough to climb the ladder the hard way. Now Buzz and me, we're cats of the same color. We got jazz in our fingers, and the hunger, the rage and the frustration in our brain. So what do we do about it? We let it come out, screaming, through our fingertips. And when it's said, we're empty. That's the end until it all builds up again. Buzz and me are punks and we'll always be punks. Our only escape is in the weed or the white stuff."

"And Johnnie Lacy?"

"He believes in things. He believes in himself, in jazz, even in cats like me. Sometimes Johnnie can almost make me believe I'm a real person instead of a perambulating nightmare. He's after me to take the cure again."

"The cure?"

"Yeah. I know you're a square, Diane. But I thought you was hip enough to know what I am—a guy on the hook, a junkie, with hell always eight hours away. The cure—sure, I've taken it twice. With Johnnie Lacey footing the bills. Each time I thought I was going to make the grade. But pretty soon something comes along that's too tough to take. A shot—just a tiny shot—and you'll be over the hump. You remember the way it was with everything calm and rosy and its starts building until you got a yen you can't control."

"But Buzz? He's not—"

"Not on the hook? Not yet. But he's hitting the weed hard and pretty soon there ain't going to be no bang left in it. So what's he got to turn to but the funk?"

"I can help him. I know I can."

"Quit kidding yourself, Diane. You can't help a guy like Buzz Baxter. All you can do is get dragged down with him. You've seen the works tonight—the honkytonks, the crummy bars, the swish clubs, the hairpin joints. That's our life—Buzz's and mine, and thousands like us. We're the hipsters, the guys and dolls who came to make the big time. We were going to see our names in bright lights. We'd be famous musicians, actors, TV stars, or what have you. But we didn't have what it takes. All the same we could see the lights, live close to them. So we became pushers, muggers, hustlers, pimps. We took over Times Square and we spread out. Up to the Circle, over to Ninth and across to Sixth. That's our territory. We got the place staked off. You don't belong, Diane. I ain't nobody's uncle, but for once I'm handing out some advice. Beat feet right out of here and don't come back. Forget about Buzz Baxter. Bury him six feet deep."

"And Johnnie Lacy?"

"Johnnie's a different breed of cat. He plays the jive dives because they give him what he wants. A chance to experiment. To change a five-piece combo into a—"

Wally broke off abruptly as a figure loomed beside the table. Johnnie Lacy was grinning down at them. He slipped into a chair beside Wally and said softly, "Take it easy, man."

Wally twisted away, his face working. He said, "Cross it out. I been spilling my guts. I'm sorry."

Lacy said, "Forget it, Wally, and thanks. Now what about taking a walk? I'd like to talk to Diane."

"Sure." Wally stood up. Diane put out her hand to him but he didn't notice. He gave a crooked grin and turned away; not toward the door but back to the washroom. Diane knew why. He'd be needing another fix.

Johnnie Lacy's face was grave. He said softly, "Wally's okay. Someday he'll take the cure for good. Then he'll make the grade."

Diane studied his face. "Why'd you send Wally after me?"

"Chip told me you were looking for Buzz. You'd never find him on your own. And looking in the wrong places could be dangerous. Anyway, Buzz won't be coming tonight. So what about letting me take you home?"

Diane said in quick alarm, "How do you know Buzz won't come? Has something happened to him?"

"Not that I know of. I just meant it's late. And Buzz is making himself scarce."

"Because of Nucci?"

"How much do you know about Nucci, Diane?"

She began to talk, telling Johnnie about Nucci. As her words poured out, the panic that had been drowned in her futile search for Buzz sprang to life again. She seemed to see Nucci's gray face as it had peered up at her window the night before, to feel the whipcord tautness of his arms as he'd held her close to him in the basement of the drugstore.

When she had finished, Johnnie said, "Maybe things aren't as bad as they look. There are ways of handling guys like Nucci."

"But Buzz—"

"I know what you're thinking. Buzz can't afford to mess with the cops. That's not what I had in mind. I'll trace Buzz down and have a talk with him. Together we can work things out. But let's lay it on the line, Diane. You're the one who's in danger. As long as Nucci's got a yen for you, you don't need to worry much about Buzz. But for you to run around on the loose with Nucci mooching about is asking for trouble. Come on, kid, I'm taking you home."

Diane bit her lip. Then she got up and let him lead her out of the restaurant. On the street, Johnnie flagged a cab. He piled in beside her but she moved away. She held herself stiffly, looking out the window at the deserted, littered streets. Johnnie watched her, smoking.

At the hotel she got out quickly, but Johnnie was beside her. He insisted on going upstairs with her. She unlocked the door and looked up at him. He started to speak but she held her finger up to her lips to silence him.

He put his hands on her arms and whispered hoarsely, "You don't know what you're mixing up in, Diane. Buzz is double trouble."

She held herself stiffly, without answering.

Johnnie's eyes searched her face. "Okay, Diane, I know what you're thinking, that I'm trying to beat Buzz's time. Maybe you're right. But I know the score and right now Buzz is top banana on your billing. But maybe it won't always be that way. Some time you may be wanting some help. When you do, call on Johnnie Lacy."

He spun around and walked away. She didn't look after him. She slipped into the foyer and leaned against the closed door. Her mother's bedside lamp spread a pale glow along the narrow corridor. Diane listened to the ragged breathing that told her that her mother had fallen asleep. There was no other sound except the soft tap of Johnnie's receding footsteps.

## 11

Buzz blinked as he stepped out into the bright sunlight of Fifth Avenue. He hadn't been up this early for a dog's age. But he'd wanted to get out of Maintree's place before she came down off her high. His fingers riffled over the roll of bills in his pocket. When he'd gotten round to counting the folding stuff he'd lifted from Maintree's purse, he'd found that it amounted to a hundred and eighty bucks. He'd been disappointed at first. He'd thought there was more in the roll. Even so, a hundred and eighty bucks was heavy sugar. Add it to the commission he'd made on his rounds and he was sitting pretty. Besides that, he'd taken a look around before he shoved off. He'd picked up a couple of rings that looked like real ice, and a jeweled watch. The way the uncles in the pawn shops gypped you, he couldn't expect much on the jewelry. But even so, the loot ought to rate a couple of dime notes.

As he reached the corner, he craned his neck to look up at Maintree's window. He didn't need to worry. The way she'd been shooting up last night, she'd be enjoying her pipe dreams for hours to come. He grinned, thinking of the fit she'd throw when she found her stuff missing. But what could she do about it? She couldn't even be sure that it was he who'd grabbed her roll. She'd been so stoned last night, she probably couldn't remember what happened.

He'd played it smart. When he lit out, he'd taken care to see that the door to her place was open. That way she couldn't ever tell but what someone else had come snooping around after he'd gone. Anyway, no matter how suspicious she was, she wouldn't dare squawk to the nabs. Not Maintree. She wouldn't want any cops sniffing around her pad.

Buzz kept on walking down the Avenue. The morning air was fresh and crisp and it gave him a lift. For a moment he thought of how he'd almost burned a fuse last night. It just showed you that you had to watch yourself all the time. But he'd pulled himself together, done what he had to do. Yeah, he'd done all right, he congratulated himself. He wondered what the cats at the Green Elephant would think when they learned he'd spent a night with Gladys Maintree. Probably they wouldn't believe him. And come to think of it, he'd better keep his lip zipped, at least while he was walking around with the swag in his pocket.

He'd been ambling along aimlessly. But that wouldn't do. He'd better put his thinking cap on. Yeah, he'd have to do some heavy brain work. For one thing, Spasm was going to be sore that he hadn't reported back last night. But he ought to be able to get around Spasm by slipping him an extra ten spot. Besides, he had a good excuse. He could say that Nucci was hanging around the entrance of Spasm's hotel and he was afraid of being highjacked. That was something a cat like Spasm could understand.

Nucci—that was the real problem. Maybe he could frame him again with the cops. But it wouldn't be easy a second time, and if word leaked out that he was a stoolie, he might as well be dead.

With Nucci in his hair, maybe he ought to speed things up with Diane. He should have called her last night, but he'd had too much on his mind. Anyway he didn't want to appear overeager or Diane might start getting ideas that she could hold out on him. She was a square, but she wasn't stupid. By now she must have a pretty good idea of the racket he was in. But that wouldn't matter, not so long as she thought he was trying to step out. Even having Nucci on his tail was good from one point of view. It gave him a chance to make some noble gestures. A mixed-up little trim like Diane would stick to a guy in trouble. Yeah, she'd get her kicks real square. A spasm of hatred passed through him, threaded with desire. That wasn't good. He'd have to play it cool all the time, remember that Diane was his ticket to the big time, that she was Willis Griscom's daughter.

He'd call her pretty soon and make a date for tonight. But not yet. It felt too good just strolling along with plenty of green stuff in his pocket. In a little while he'd duck into a barber shop in one of the swanky hotels and buy himself a haircut and a shave. Maybe a manicure too. Why not? The cats in the know claimed that big shots made half their contacts in hotel barber shops. It was time Buzz started practicing up. Pretty soon he'd be up there with the big boys. Then he wouldn't have to worry about a small-time goon like Nucci.

At the thought of Nucci he automatically looked over his shoulder, even though he knew it was crazy. A zombie like Nucci wouldn't stick his face out of doors until after it was dark. A picture of Nucci, sprawled out, half-dressed, across a cot popped into Buzz's mind. It was funny how he happened to know where Nucci was shacking up. Usually a guy like Nucci would be careful not to let information like that out of the bag. But when Nucci had been sprung, he needed a switchblade quick. Nucci would feel naked if he had to go out in the streets without a springer in his pocket. So he'd bought one from a Puerto Rican who used to play in Johnnie's band. The Puerto Rican had delivered the shank to an address on 116th Street, and when he'd seen Buzz last night, he'd told him about the deal and warned him to keep out of Nucci's path.

Buzz decided not to get his shave after all. At least not until he'd squared things with Spasm. He hailed a cab and leaned back, taking it easy, until he got to Spasm's place.

After he got through with Spasm he was too bushed even to think of a barber shop. The little cripple was in a nasty mood, and the dime note hadn't sweetened him up at all. Spasm had laid down the law. Either Buzz would toe the line, get the money back on the same night, or Spasm would hire himself a new boy. Buzz had got red-headed and let himself run off at the mouth. That was a mistake, and he knew it just as soon as Spasm slammed the door on him. He would have felt a lot worse if the folding stuff he'd lifted from Gladys Maintree hadn't been nestling in his pocket.

Even so, as soon as he cooled off, he realized he was on the dime. Maintree couldn't afford to turn in a squeal as long as he was her lifeline to the white stuff. But what would happen when she learned Buzz wasn't working for the syndicate any longer? He couldn't be sure and he didn't dare take any chances. He'd better get rid of the jewelry quick, even if he had to toss it in an ashcan. He saw a trey of knockers in the next block and started toward it but halfway there he changed his mind and headed for the subway instead.

By the time he got back to his pad he could hardly keep his eyes open. He started to strip off his clothes, and then he saw Dottie had been camping in his place. There were fresh roaches in the ashtray and the coffee cup on the table was smeared with her lipstick. He'd hoped that he was through with her. Next time she came around, he was going to kick her tail out of here once and for all. But that could wait. He threw himself down on the bed and lit a reefer. He was on the nod before he finished. He had just enough sense to snuff out the roach before he closed his eyes.

He thought he had slept for only a few minutes, but it was dusk when the steady tattoo of knuckles on the door awakened him. He leapt up in instant alarm, then stood still, listening. Could it be Nucci? No, he wouldn't come so openly. Dottie? She would have tried her key. The nabs then? He remembered the rings and the jeweled watch in his pocket. He ought to get out, through the window, into the mews and over the fence.

"Buzz, open up, will you?" The voice sounded familiar, but he couldn't place it immediately.

He moved cautiously to the door. "Who is it?"

"Me. Johnnie Lacy."

Buzz let out a sigh of relief. He didn't know how Johnnie had smelled him out. Through Dottie, probably. He'd really have to lace into that trim when he got hold of her. He took the guard chain off and opened the door for Johnnie.

Buzz grinned but Johnnie's face was solemn, set in hard lines. Buzz asked, "What's dangling?"

"Plenty. Where were you last night?"

"Hey, Johnnie, you know better'n to ask questions like that."

"Yeah, I imagine so. But Diane was looking for you all over the turf."

"The crazy little frill. What'd she want to do that for?"

"She's not crazy, Buzz. She's in love with you."

"Sure. My fatal charm."

"Cut out the wisecracks, Buzz. This is serious."

"For God's sake, what gives? You act like you was gone on her yourself. You ain't tryin' to poach on me, are you, man?"

Johnnie's fist knotted and Buzz took an instinctive step backward. He didn't want to rumble with Johnnie. He said placatingly, "Cool it, man. I was talking through my toupee."

Johnnie relaxed a little but not much. He said softly, "The kid's in a mess."

"Yeah?"

"Nucci caught up with her last night. He wants to make a deal. If Diane will play along with him, he'll forget about our taking over his route."

Buzz whistled and his eyes narrowed. He was thinking fast, but he didn't want Johnnie to get an inkling of his thoughts.

Johnnie kept on talking. "You know Nucci's record. A term for rape number one. A couple other rape charges that folded up. Half a dozen slicings. Narcotics. Pimping. The guy's a psycho and on the needle to boot."

"Sure, I know."

"Do you know where he's catting up?"

Buzz hesitated for a moment. There wasn't any sense handing out any free info to Johnnie. He shook his head then he asked cautiously, "What's on your mind?"

"If you and I could reach him, maybe we could talk some sense into him. And if we can't, between us we ought to be able to handle him."

Buzz's lips twisted. "Did you ever use a shank or brass knucks, Johnnie?"

"I've never had to."

"Nucci don't fight by the rules. Anyway, what good would beating him up do? He wouldn't just punk out. He'd be after blood."

"The cops, then."

"Man, you're not talking sense. You think the cops are going to lock him up and throw away the key on your say-so? And what if they do pinch him? Pretty soon the word would get around we fingered him. Then we'd all be dead ducks—you, me, and Diane."

"We've got to try it."

"You ain't got to try nothing, Johnnie. This is my pigeon, not yours. I got a way of handling Nucci. It'll work, too, if you don't foul things up."

Johnnie said fiercely, "I don't trust you, Buzz. One thing you got to promise—you'll keep Diane in the clear."

"Look, Johnnie, your concern for my trim is very touching. But why don't you play hero somewhere else? Me, I got things to attend to."

Johnnie took a step toward him. He said, "Okay, Buzz, but I'm warning you—"

Buzz didn't back away this time. He'd reached for the table where his switchblade lay. The shank gave him courage and he made his voice tough. "Suppose you do the listening, Johnnie. You ain't warnin' me about nothin'. You're getting the hell out of here, pronto."

Johnnie stood still, and Buzz could see the muscles around his jaws working. For a minute he thought he'd let himself in for a hassle. He'd thought Johnnie was soft. But looking at him now he wasn't so sure. There was something fanatical in the guy's eyes. Buzz eased up, managed a grin. He said, "Take it easy, Johnnie. I was just tryin' to tell you, I got my own plans. You wouldn't want to screw things up for Diane, would you?"

"Give her a break, Buzz. Leave her alone."

Buzz could have burst out laughing then. The guy

was really dreamy over Diane. But he didn't stand a show with her—not with Buzz Baxter around. What's more, he had Johnnie by the short hairs. The jerk wouldn't dare try anything for fear that Buzz would take it out on Diane, give her a rough time.

Buzz leaned back against the wall, playing it cool. "You wouldn't want to make me sore, would you? You wouldn't want nothin' to happen to Diane. So be a good guy, will you? Broom off."

# 12

After Johnnie had left, Buzz stood by the door thinking. So Nucci had hot pants over Diane. That was a laugh, a good big loud one. Imagine a goon like Nucci thinking he could make time with Diane. Buzz wiped his mouth with the back of his hand. This was going to be good. He wasn't without a weapon any longer. He had something Nucci wanted. Yeah, Diane could pay off in more ways than one.

He was feeling lightheaded. He hadn't realized how Nucci was getting on his nerves. But now he didn't have to worry any longer. Nucci wouldn't be slicing him up, not with Diane dangling in front of his eyes. His brain was really clicking, he thought, clear as a bell. The plan that was evolving in his mind sounded foolproof, but there were a lot of angles that needed his attention. He'd have to be careful and lay off the weed too. The weed gave you too much confidence, so you goofed things right at the time when you should proceed with caution.

He took a shower, letting the lukewarm water spray over him for nearly ten minutes. He shaved and dressed, selecting his clothes with care—charcoal-gray slacks, a fresh white shirt, a maroon tie. He picked up his tweed jacket, then decided against it. There was a chance he'd be seeing action tonight. The leather windbreaker would give him more freedom. He put it on and slipped the switchblade into the slit pocket.

He checked his watch. He had time, oceans of it. Anyway, he was the guy who was calling the shots now. Nucci would be slavering all over him before the night was out. He began to hum a tune. He reached for the jacket he'd worn last night and dug the diamond rings out of the inside pocket. The stones had a deep glow that was almost like a solid flame. If any uncle tried to tell him they were phonies, he'd walk out.

He tried on his gray fedora in front of the mirror, adjusting the brim so that it shaded his eyes. He had everything all set in his own mind. If the plan wasn't perfect, it was damn close to it. He let himself out onto the street, walking jauntily. It was a good feeling, not having to duck Nucci any longer. Pretty soon he'd be looking him up.

He bought a paper from the stand in front of the subway kiosk. There was a greasy spoon on the corner. He'd better stoke up on some food. Hell, he'd been practically living on reefers and coffee the last few days. He went in, ordered a couple of hamburgers and a glass of milk and took them to a corner table. He unfolded the paper and began skimming through the headlines.

He was almost finished eating when the story caught his eye. It was only a few inches, tucked down at the bottom of the page. He'd passed over it once without its registering, then he did a quick double-take. The headline announced: ACTRESS ROBBED IN FIFTH AVENUE APARTMENT.

He read on:

Gladys Maintree, well-known star of stage and screen, was a victim of robbery early this morning. According to the police, Miss Maintree awakened to find a man prowling through her bedroom. She screamed and the marauder fled but she was able to identify him as Luis Mercado, an elevator operator in the employ of the apartment house. Mercado was apprehended two hours later in his home. Several pieces of Miss Maintree's jewelry were found concealed in his room. Two valuable rings, a watch and about eight hundred dollars in cash, however, were not recovered.

Buzz read the story over again, trying to fill in the picture. He remembered the smirk Luis had given him early this morning when he'd left Maintree's place. Right then Buzz knew he should have walked down to the street. But sixteen flights was too much after a hard night.

After Luis had let Buzz out, he must have gone back to Maintree's apartment to see what was up. He'd found the door open and probably decided it was safe to snoop around and pick up anything that would stick to his fingers, because when Maintree came off her jag she'd be sure to blame the theft on Buzz. Yeah, the kid had tried to put a frame around him and the only reason it hadn't worked was because Maintree had awakened at the wrong moment.

At first Buzz wanted to laugh, then a new idea hit him and sobered him up quick. The cops had hold of

Luis, and as soon as they started putting pressure on him he'd run off at his mouth about Buzz being there last night. Maybe the cops wouldn't believe him, but they'd start checking. And Buzz couldn't afford a checkup. Especially not with the loot in his pocket.

Buzz began to sweat. He'd thought he was clear with Gladys Maintree. She wouldn't call the cops on him because he could turn the tables on her, spill about the junk she had stashed in her place. Besides that, he might cut off her connections. But Maintree hadn't been afraid to call copper on a little punk like Luis. She'd reckon he couldn't do her any harm.

So where did that leave Buzz? Luis must have picked up a few gadgets that Buzz hadn't thought were worth snagging. The cops had found those on him. But they had a description of the rings and the watch. They probably reckoned Luis was lying, that he'd passed on the loot to someone else. Their first step would be to put out a tracer, circulate it around the pawnshops. By night there wouldn't be an uncle in town who didn't know the ice was hot.

Buzz read over the part of the story where Maintree claimed to have lost eight C's. That was easy to explain. She was trying to nick the insurance company for some extra sugar. Buzz started wondering about Luis again. Had the punk ever been around when Maintree called him Buzz? He didn't think so. But Luis knew he was a pusher and would be able to give a description of him. But the chances were heavy against the nabs swallowing the punk's story. They'd think it was something he dreamed up. Just the same, they might pass the word along to the narcotics squad. Anyone who was hip could tell Maintree was on the main line by taking half a look.

Buzz's hands were trembling so that the paper rattled. He'd felt so safe a few minutes ago. He'd had the world by the tail. And now a little jerk like Luis was spoiling everything. Suddenly he felt like bawling. Every time he arranged the perfect setup, someone came along to trip him. He got up quickly. The panic was in him again, squeezing at the muscles of his stomach, making sweat sprout out on the back of his hands. He wanted to run through the streets to try to keep ahead of the danger that was always at his heels. But that wouldn't do. He had to go ahead with his plan. But now he'd have to speed up the schedule.

He grabbed his hat and strode to the door. He was almost running when he hit the entrance to the subway kiosk. Just as he reached the first step, a hand clamped onto his arm, spun him around. Buzz wanted to scream but he fought silently, trying to free himself of the viselike grip. He jerked loose but lost his balance and sprawled across the railing. Before he could straighten up the man was standing over him. Buzz looked at him with frightened eyes. He wasn't a cop, and not Nucci, either. What the hell did he want?

The guy was babbling in broken English. The only words that Buzz caught were eighty-five cents. Suddenly Buzz realized who he was—the cashier at the greasy spoon. Buzz didn't know whether to be sore or to laugh. He'd forgotten to pay for the hamburgers and milk. All the same if this stud should decide to call the cops, he could be in a hole. He'd better play it cool.

He managed to get his hand in his pocket and drag out some bills. There was a fin on top and he pushed it into the guy's hand. He said, "For God's sake, did you think I was running out on a measly eighty-five-cent take? I was just busy thinking. Take the five and forget it, will you?"

The cashier took the bill and folded it up. He was still mumbling, but he didn't interfere when Buzz slipped by him, down the subway steps. Buzz was moving fast now, shaking all over. He was so rattled he could hardly poke his token into the slot of the turnstile. That was bad, because if things were to go right, he'd need a clear head. He leaned up against a pillar and let the first train go by. He'd planned to lay off the weed, but right now what he needed was a little gauge to take the edge off his nerves. He found the washroom, went into a cubicle and lit up. The pack he'd bought last night was real Mex, light brown, smooth as honey. It reached him in no time flat. By the time he'd finished the stick, he was on the ball again, ready to ride.

He jostled his way into the next uptown train and found a seat at the end of the car. He was still riding the broom and he gave a start of surprise when he looked up and saw that the train was stopped at 125th Street. He reached the door just as it was closing, and squeezed through.

He passed the pawnshop the first time without spotting it, and had to turn back. He'd been there once with one of the boys from the band, but he'd got the idea that the cat who ran it was cop-shy. The place was a hole in the wall, with junk piled high in the single window so that you couldn't see inside. He peered through the grimy door. A single bulb at the back and a gooseneck on an old-fashioned desk gave the interior a curious brown illumination.

A bell tinkled as he opened the door. A little man straightened up from behind the counter. He had a pale, round, expressionless face and a bulging forehead. He stared at Buzz without speaking. Something about his impassive look disconcerted Buzz. What if he had this guy wrong? What if he should yell copper? Maybe the thing to do was to walk right out again. But then he'd have to find another place.

He'd planned to spill a story. But what was the use? This guy would know the ice was hot. He tossed the two rings down on a little purple velvet mat on top of the counter. The man picked them up, carried them to the desk and examined them in the light of the gooseneck. He took a long time and Buzz was getting jittery. He'd read somewhere that some pawnbrokers could push a button to summon the nabs. Could the guy be stalling to give the cops a chance to show on the scene?

Buzz's fingers drummed on the counter. He was listening so hard for signs of danger from the street that he didn't hear the man come back toward him until the rings clattered on the glass. He was sweating and he knew that that was a dead giveaway. Why didn't this zombie say something? Name a price?

"How much?"

The little man spread his hands expressively. His voice came out gently, with a slight lisp. "Nice—but dangerous. The police ask so many questions."

The stud was threatening him, Buzz realized, warning him that if he tried to walk out now the cops would be on his tail.

"How much?" he repeated hoarsely.

"Thirty dollars."

Buzz's jaw tightened. "You know where you can shove that thirty dollars."

The man's lips twitched. "If you think you can do better, go somewhere else. But—" He let the threat drop.

Buzz understood all right. If he went out of here with the rings he'd probably be collared before he'd made the next block. And even if he wasn't, he'd be on the run. That was something he couldn't afford. He forced his voice back to normal. "What about a trade?"

The man's shoulder lifted, "What would you suggest?"

"A rod."

"Unlicensed, they come high."

"So do diamonds."

The man stood still for a moment, then went to the back of the shop. When he returned there was a small, snub-nosed .32 in his hand. He placed it beside the rings.

Buzz hefted the revolver. It was light, compact, and looked efficient. He broke it open and saw that it was empty. "It's no good to me unless it's loaded."

The man hesitated, then he picked up the rings and carried them to his desk. When he came back he spilled six bullets across the counter. Buzz snatched them up. The man was saying something, but he didn't listen. He wanted to get out, and fast.

As soon as he was outside, he saw a prowl car crawling along the block. He fought the impulse to duck into a doorway. It was the worst thing he could do. He steeled himself to keep a steady pace, but his knees seemed to have turned to water. A wave of self-pity swept over him. Nothing was going right. Luis, the crazy cashier, the zombie in the pawnshop, they were all trying to foul him up. But he'd fool them and after tonight he'd be sitting up on top where nobody could touch him.

He still had a lot of things to do but first of all he'd better put distance between himself and the pawnshop. The guy back there with his soft lisping voice gave him the creeps. Maybe as soon as Buzz was gone, he'd pulled a double-cross and phoned the cops. It would be a hell of a note, Buzz thought, if he should get picked up with a rod on him. There was the stolen watch, too. He'd planned to make a separate deal with the watch but he'd forgotten all about it in his eagerness to get away.

He'd had all he could stomach of pawnshops anyhow. He'd ditch the watch the first chance he got. He could toss it into the wire trash basket on the corner, but somebody might spot him. Then he had another idea and he grinned to himself. He'd really fix Luis's wagon. But he'd work that out later.

He hailed a cab and told the driver to take him downtown. But then he began thinking about Nucci. If he missed contact with Nucci tonight, he'd have to postpone the whole plan for another twenty-four hours, and with a few more setbacks, he might lose his nerve. He'd better get Nucci fast. It was just beginning to get dark and the guy would probably still be at his pad.

The taxi was entering Central Park and Buzz told the driver to swing around and take him back to 116th. He got out a couple of blocks from where Nucci was shacking up. He began walking along slowly, watching the numbers on the fanlights. He'd thought it was going to be easy selling this deal to Nucci, but now he wasn't so sure. Nucci was smart even if he was a junkie. He might smell a trap. And what would he do then? He was glad he had the gun along, even though it wasn't time to use it yet. He found a back alley that led to a condemned tenement. He slipped in and fitted the bullets into the chamber. The feel of the gun in the pocket of his windbreaker should have given him confidence, but it seemed only to weigh him down. Just having it there was an admission that he still had to fear Nucci's knife.

He found the number, a narrow three-story brownstone wedged in between two almost identical buildings. A high stoop with a rusted iron railing brought him to a smudged glass door that hung askew. The hallway was dark, redolent with the smells of garlic and rancid fat. There were no names anywhere, no markings on the door. People who lived in a rattrap like this didn't advertise their presence.

The Puerto Rican kid had told Buzz where Nucci's room was. Second floor back, the last door to the right. Buzz started climbing the worn wooden stairway. Each step squealed in protest as it took his weight. Buzz grinned to himself. No need for doorbells here. Nobody upstairs could be taken by surprise. A door opened on the landing above and the nasal twang of a Spanish-speaking announcer became a roar. The voice stopped and the music of a dance band echoed through the bare, narrow corridor.

A man's figure was silhouetted in an open doorway. The glaring light behind him blanked out his features, accentuated the narrow shoulders, the thin body. Buzz gave him a single glance, then moved on down the hallway toward Nucci's room. The loose boards cracked and groaned beneath his feet, but the feverish, high-pitched music of the band deadened all other sounds.

Buzz knocked and when there was no answer pounded hard on the flimsy panel. Nucci could be on the nod and if he was it would take a lot of noise to snap him out of it. There was still no response. Buzz rattled the door, gave it a couple of kicks. Either Nucci wasn't home, or he was really stoned.

Buzz turned and saw that the man behind him had moved out of the doorway into the hall. He'd lit up and Buzz knew by the red glow that the cigarette was a reefer. Buzz walked toward him and stopped at the head of the stairs.

The man's voice was thin, reedy. "You lookin' for somebody, pal?"

"What d'you think I'm doing—shadow boxing?"

"Who cares?"

Buzz tried to make out his features, but there was only the red glow in the black mask. Then the man asked tonelessly, "The name wouldn't be Baxter, would it?"

Buzz's hand clenched over the splintered wood of the railing. Who the hell was this cat? What did he want? He remained silent, feeling his breath suck in hard.

"Yeah," the man said, "I guess you're Baxter. I got a message for you. Frank's in the poolroom on the corner. He's expectin' you." He swung around abruptly and went in through the lighted doorway, slamming the door after him.

Buzz stood still in the darkness, trying to figure out the next move. He'd been suckered plenty. It hadn't been any coincidence that the Puerto Rican kid had dropped around to tell him where Nucci was shacked up. Nucci had planned it that way, had probably slipped the kid a buck to pass on the information: That meant that Nucci had been sure he'd make a quick deal, that he'd sell out Diane to get out from under.

It could mean a double-cross, too. Maybe Nucci didn't have a yen for Diane after all. Buzz had heard that cats who'd been on the white stuff as long as Nucci lost their male, didn't give a damn about women. So Nucci could be setting a trap and Buzz would be walking right into it if he went to the poolroom. But it was a chance he'd have to take. He couldn't be dodging Nucci's knife forever. The guy was a weirdie, a psycho. You couldn't tell what he might pull.

Buzz hunched his shoulders and started down the stairs. He moved slowly, cautiously, listening for some sign of danger. He wished the guy up above would cut down on the volume of the radio. If Nucci was really laying for him, what better place would there be than these dark, narrow stairs?

He was breathing hard by the time he hit the street. But he might have saved his breath. He hadn't met anyone on the stairs or in the foyer. He looked around for the poolroom. It was easy enough to spot. A long window smeared over with yellow paint. A sign above it: Corazon de Ponce—Pool—Billiards. The click of balls and the sounds of raucous laughter poured out through an open door.

He stood in the doorway, steeling himself to enter. A gang of teenage punks dressed in peg-leg pants and striped jerseys surrounded the nearest table. They were chattering in high-pitched Puerto Rican Spanish. One of them looked up, saw him and hissed. The others turned to look at him and the room grew silent.

Buzz saw Nucci. He was alone at the far table, sighting along the cue. His arm drew back and there was a sharp crack, followed by the muted thunder of the balls rolling across the table. He straightened up and chalked his cue. His pale gray eyes swept across Buzz, but he gave no sign of recognition. He crouched again and neatly pocketed the six-ball.

Buzz crossed over to the table. "I hear you're expecting me."

"Yeah. I thought you'd be along."

"You want to make a deal?"

"Sure, I told sugar-puss all about it. I guess she reckons you won't play. She thinks you're noble."

Buzz stared at him, hating him. But he kept his voice harsh, toneless. "Maybe I can fix things up. We got some talking to do."

"Sure, and these studs around here got big ears. Come on."

Nucci led the way to the rear, where there was a stairway leading to the basement. Buzz hesitated at the top. He was taking a chance going down there alone with Nucci. But it was better than jaw-blocking in the open poolroom. The fewer people who saw him with Nucci tonight, the better.

Nucci turned bleak eyes upon him and his colorless lips curled in a contemptuous smile. Buzz knew what Nucci was thinking—that he was yellow. He gritted his teeth. "What are you waiting for?"

Nucci started down the stairs, and Buzz followed. Buzz could feel the solid weight of the revolver in his wind-breaker pocket. It would be easy, he thought, to shoot Nucci in the back, then beat feet out of here. But that was plain crazy, ringing the gong, setting himself up for the chair.

Play it cool, man, he told himself. Stick to the plan. Wait till you get this crud right where you want him before you give him the works.

# 13

The waiting today had been worse than that of yesterday. Diane felt the quivering tautness of her body as hour after hour passed with no word from Buzz. He simply had to call her soon. Something had been broken, left jagged and unfinished, as when music stopped in the middle of a chord and the unexpected silence became unbearable. That's the way it was with her and Buzz. Something had begun between them, then come to a sudden stop. Somehow she had to see him, bring to some conclusion the pattern of their relationship.

She tried to envision Buzz's face, the hard, lean features, the mocking yet frightened eyes. She imagined him in flight, from Nucci, from himself. And she ran beside him, with neon lights flashing about them and the sounds and smells of Times Square enveloping them.

She went to the window. A narrow ledge girded the side of the building. In her mind she stood on the coping, fighting the impulse to plunge downward to her destruction. What did she want? Was she in love with Buzz? Or did he fulfill some need within her— the relief from tension, the craving for escape?

Behind her she heard her mother come to the door, but she did not turn. She had no desire to resume the bitter, meaningless quarrel of the early afternoon. She had won her victory and her mother had dissolved in helpless tears. She had cut herself loose from the soft, smothering cords with which her mother had bound her. She was free, but what good was her freedom without Buzz? She had to see him, be with him, to make sure of her escape.

The phone shrilled. She hurried to it, swooping it up. But it wasn't Buzz. The clear, steady tones were those of Johnnie Lacy. He said, "Hi, Diane. Have you heard from Buzz yet?"

"No. Did you see him?"

"Yeah, quite a while back. I told him about Nucci, about how he'd threatened you."

"What did he say?"

"Not much." Johnnie's voice was guarded. "He just seemed to take it in his stride."

"Is Buzz all right? Did Nucci—"

Johnnie broke in impatiently. "Look, Diane, can't you get it into your head that you're the one that Nucci's after? It's you who's on the spot."

"But Buzz—"

Johnnie's voice came riding over hers. "I'm going to hand it to you straight. Buzz acted relieved, almost pleased. He's got some trick up his sleeve. I don't know what it is, but Buzz may try to use you for bait, Diane. Don't let him."

"He wouldn't do that."

"No? How much do you know about Buzz Baxter? Do you—"

She laid the instrument down, refusing to listen. How could Johnnie Lacy understand about her need for Buzz? Johnnie was of no more help to her than her mother was.

She was still waiting for Buzz when Johnnie called again. She fought to conceal her irritation and her disappointment. Why couldn't Johnnie leave her alone? Even while he was talking Buzz might be trying to get through to her.

Johnnie's manner was contrite. He said, "Maybe I was all wet about Buzz. Maybe he's on the level after all."

How could she make Johnnie understand that that wasn't what mattered? How could she tell him of something about which she herself had only a vague understanding? Buzz's fierce, undirected anger, his harshness, his lack of control touched off these same qualities in her, gave meaning and fire to her restless discontent.

There wasn't any sense in trying to explain these things to Johnnie. She said coolly, "Thanks for everything, Johnnie. But you don't have to worry about me."

Johnnie was silent for a moment. Then he spoke quickly, his words tumbling over one another. "Diane, I don't think Buzz is going to show tonight. But me, I'm free as a bird. I got someone to fill in on the piano and I got nothing to do but sit on my hands. So what about taking in a jam session somewhere? Maybe at Birdland?"

"You know I can't."

"I guess not. But sitting alone waiting for Buzz is no good. Let me come to the hotel and wait with you."

"You're sweet, Johnnie. But it's still no."

He tried to keep it light but he couldn't conceal the hurt in his voice. "Okay, Diane, I give up. But no one can say I didn't try. And as I told you last night, if you're in trouble, I'm your boy."

She had hardly hung up when the phone peeled again. This time it was Buzz. The sound of his voice sent excitement racing through her. The hours of waiting seemed to shrink into nothingness. She cried, "Buzz! I tried to find you all last night. Nucci was—"

He cut her off, his voice gruff. "Yeah, I know all about that. Johnnie was up to my place, making like Sir Galahad. What gives between you two?"

"Nothing, Buzz."

"Okay, forget it. But keep that stud out of my hair. I know how to deal with Nucci. You don't have to worry about that bum. I paid him off—a hundred bucks. A C-note, that was all the louse wanted. Now he's got it and to hell with him. Cross him out of your mind."

"But Buzz, Nucci said—"

"Sure, I know what he said. He was trying to throw a scare into you, that's all. But I didn't call you up to jaw-block about Nucci. How about you and me getting close tonight? We could meet the same place, the same time."

A picture flashed through her mind of the penny arcade, the jostling crowd that hung around the entrance. Maybe Nucci would be among them, his gray face turned to her, watching with his expressionless eyes.

"Couldn't it be somewhere else?"

"Hey, baby, what's the matter with you? You turned chicken or something?"

"I'll be there, Buzz."

"That's better. I'll get there early just in case some stud might get ideas if he sees you hanging around."

She heard the sharp click of the receiver as he hung up. She stood holding the instrument in her hand for a few moments, her thoughts rebellious. What if she didn't show? What if she stood him up? It would serve him right. But what was the sense of thinking like that? She'd be there and she'd be there on time. Because if she wasn't, he might not wait, and she couldn't risk that.

Buzz stepped out of the telephone booth, a sardonic grin twisting his lips. Nucci was right where he'd left him at the end of the row of booths, the pale light showing on his parchment-like face. The zombie was really working himself up a sweat.

Nucci grabbed hold of the sleeve of his windbreaker. "Did you fix it up, Buzz?" he asked hoarsely.

"It was a snap. I told you the trim goes for me in a big way."

"She's fancy stuff. Maybe she won't play."

"Stow it, man. She's eating out of my hand." Buzz dug a key out of his pocket and thrust it into Nucci's palm. "You do like I tell you, and it will be easy as rolling off a log. But you gotta keep outa sight until I get her inside. Then she's all yours."

Nucci's eyes narrowed. "You wouldn't be thinkin' of crossin' me, Buzz? You ain't forgot what I can do with a slicer?"

"Man, you're talking crazy. What's a piece of lace to me?"

Buzz watched Nucci shamble off with his strange, loping gate. Did the crazy goon really think Buzz was going to play his game? His fingers touched the revolver tucked in the pocket of his windbreaker and he had to laugh. Tonight, if things went right, he'd be the fair-haired boy, the guy who'd saved Willis Griscom's daughter from being raped by a stir-crazy sex fiend. Yeah, he'd be a hero and Nucci'd be dead.

The setup was perfect. All he had to do was get Diane to his pad and if he knew the score, that was going to be easy. Nucci would be in the closet hiding. After a couple of minutes Buzz would excuse himself, saying he was going out for some cigarettes or sandwiches. He'd leave, slamming the door. That would be the signal to Nucci that the coast was clear.

Yeah, that's what Nucci thought. But Buzz had plans of his own. He was going to stay right outside the door. He'd give Nucci time to muss Diane up, rip her dress, bruise her arms. Then Buzz would come popping right back in and Nucci wouldn't have a chance to use his shank because Buzz would shoot first. And when he did he was going to make sure that it was curtains for Nucci.

So by tomorrow Frank Nucci would be off his shoulders for good, with a couple of bullet holes in him. And who was going to blame Buzz when he'd caught Nucci red-handed mauling his girl? The cops weren't going to ask too many questions, not about a psycho like Nucci with a record for dope-peddling and rape. Nobody was likely to shed a tear over the bum, least of all the cops. They'd probably be glad to pin a medal on his killer.

The only hole in the plan that Buzz could spot was the gun. He didn't have a license and the nabs could book him on a Sullivan Law violation. But that was where Griscom would come in. A guy like Griscom could throw a lot of weight and he ought to be plenty grateful to a cat who'd saved his daughter from a rapist. Yeah, Buzz ought to be in plenty solid with Griscom. And more than anything else, Griscom would want to keep things nice and quiet. A guy who fronted for the syndicate had to play it careful. Respectability was more important to him than to a priest or a college professor. The front had to be beyond reproach, lily-white.

Buzz strolled out onto 116th Street. Nucci was already out of sight. Buzz felt like laughing, thinking of Nucci and the big surprise in store for him. How stupid could a guy get? And Diane was almost as dumb, playing right into his hands, eating up his story about paying Nucci off.

He began walking along, his hands in his pockets, humming a tune that he could hear being played on a jukebox nearby. Then his fingers touched something round and hard. He drew it out of his pocket. The watch he'd snagged from Maintree. He should have gotten rid of it long ago, but he'd forgotten all about it.

He felt the tingling of nerves in his fingertips. You had to watch yourself all the time or some little thing could trip you up. Tonight, when he'd shot Nucci, the cops would be sure to pat him down. And what if they came up with a stolen watch? A thing like that could screw up the whole works.

He had to get rid of the watch quick. Already Luis might have sicked the cops onto him. There was a bar and grill a few doors away. He'd go in and amble back to the washroom. Maybe he'd push the watch down among the dirty paper towels or toss it into the tank of the john.

The dive was almost empty and the bartender gave him a nod as he came in. So maybe he'd better buy himself a beer. He was drinking the stuff when he saw the envelope on the floor beside one of the booths. The envelope gave him an idea. It was plain dime-store stuff, and someone had stepped on leaving the imprint of a rubber heel. Buzz stooped and picked it up.

Nobody was paying him any mind. He smoothed the envelope on the bar and printed Luis Mercado's name in big block letters and beneath it the address of the building where Gladys Maintree lived. He wondered if Luis were still in the pokey or if he'd been able to make bail. It didn't matter; Luis wouldn't be running the elevator any longer and the chances were ten to one that whoever got the envelope would pass it to the cops. Whatever story Luis had been telling about Buzz would be blown sky-high. The nabs would reckon Luis had mailed the watch to himself or, if he was in the slammer at the time it was posted, that he had had a confederate. Yeah, Luis was going to have a lot of explaining to do.

He went back to the washroom and wrapped the watch in tissue paper before sealing it in the envelope. Outside on the next corner was a brightly lit drugstore with a stamp machine beside the cashier's cage. Buzz was feeling good as he stuck the stamps on the envelope and thrust it into a mailbox.

It was the details that counted, he told himself. Now everything was clear. Nucci, Diane, Luis—they were all like puppets, dancing when he pulled the strings. He felt a surge of power go through him. Nobody was going to stop Buzz Baxter now. The way he'd handled the matter of the watch showed his brain was really clicking on all fours. The only thing that could make him feel any better was a couple of pokes off a reefer. But he'd better lay off the sweet stuff tonight. There wasn't any sense taking chances. He was doing all right just as he was. Besides, he'd better get cracking if he was going to meet Diane on time.

## 14

The ragged syncopated rhythm of the "Honkytonk Blues" flooded the Moontime Club. But instead of sending Buzz the way it usually did, the jazz frayed at his nerves, gave him the jitters. He cast a sidelong glance at Diane sitting beside him. The murky dimness of the room highlighted her peaked cheekbones, made pools of shadows beneath them, so that her face had a still, almost distant look.

There was a change in her, something Buzz couldn't understand but which made him uneasy. Pretty soon he'd have to start pitching his line. And he'd better make it good, because if he showed up at his pad without Diane, he'd have a lot of explaining to do to Nucci. And Nucci would be in no mood to do any heavy listening. Earlier it hadn't occurred to him Diane wouldn't fall in with his plans, but now he wasn't so sure. Maybe somebody had planted a seed of suspicion in her mind. His thoughts flicked to Johnnie Lacy. Some time he was going to get that stud alone and rip his spine out and nail it to the wall.

The anger took hold of him, spread out until his skin felt too tight, ready to burst. Up on the bandstand the instruments had faded out and the cat at the piano was picking out a slow, hard rhythm that had a jarring force. Buzz wished he could take over the piano. He'd speed up the beat, let himself go wild on the eighty-eight. He'd pour out his rage on the black and whites until he was empty.

Diane was watching him and he'd have to cool it. He mustn't let his anger show, not now when he had everything lying right in his lap. He tried to grin but his face felt stiff and his eyes hot. He reached into his pocket for the reefers he had stowed there. Lighting up in front of Diane was risky but it was better than blowing his top. He heard the little pop as the gauge caught the flame. Then he inhaled, holding the smoke in his lungs, letting it out slow. Diane's eyes were still upon him but he didn't dare look at her. He twisted his head away and took another poke. Then her hand was on top of his, her fingers white against his dark skin.

He whirled on her, feeling the defenses he'd put up against his rage cracking. In a minute he'd be yelling at her. Her face was expressionless, her eyes veiled. She plucked the reefer out of his fingers and slid it between her lips. Slowly she sucked the smoke into her mouth.

He laughed then, knowing everything was going to be all right. She was telling him she was playing the game according to his rules. He stretched an arm around her and drew her to him. He kissed her and felt her lips soft beneath his. She didn't move away afterward but lifted her face so that she was looking up at him.

Everything was solid again. No need to hurry. He could let things ride, take his time. Thinking of Nucci cramped up in his closet made him grin. Let the stud sweat it out. One thing was for sure, Nucci wasn't going any place. Not while he thought there was a chance of getting his paws on Diane. So the longer Buzz waited, the better. If it was late when he brought Diane to his pad, there'd be less chance of some longnose prowling about the turf, seeing things he shouldn't see.

Buzz relaxed, letting the music take hold of him. These boys were really cool. They did a ride-out finish on a blues number and immediately slipped into "Way Down Deep." It was a colored band. They played effortlessly, with an easy rhythm, just poking along until the cornetist suddenly let loose. His head hung down and his eyes were closed but the arpeggios pulsed out of his horn like the frantic squeals of a butchered pig. The cornet subsided and the drums set a more rapid beat. The band started building up and at the end of the chorus, the cornetist picked it up again, raising his instrument this time, letting the notes soar up and up until they burst in a silver spray of sound.

Buzz pulled Diane closer. He whispered, "That cat on the horn gasses me. Man, he makes me float."

Diane's laughter tinkled. "He's good, isn't he? Really good."

Buzz felt a spasm of jealousy. Sure, these cats knew their stuff, but so did Buzz Baxter. He thought of the honky-tonks he'd played, the combos. He could make a piano sit up and talk. But who cared about that? They'd booted him out because he'd flipped his conk or got stoned or because he wouldn't take any lip from the boy on top. Nobody'd ever given him a break. So now they couldn't blame him if he made his own.

The cat on the horn had broken loose again. Buzz said slowly, "Yeah, tonight he's in the groove, but half the time when he tries the high register stuff, he hits a clinker."

Diane mocked him with her eyes but her face moved closer, awaiting his kiss. Buzz turned away, pretending not to understand. His irritability was creeping back and with it a sense of frustration. His dreams never came true. Maybe he was a cat who was meant never to get the breaks. Things always got screwed up for him and it was never his own fault. The thick smoke of the room seemed to clutch at his throat. He wanted to get outside, to be on the move.

He stood up. "Let's dangle. Let's find ourselves another spot. Maybe we can find one with some South

American flavor. Do you go for the Latin stuff?"

She spoke lazily. "I like it here. Why not wait for the next number?"

Suddenly he wanted to slap her, scream at her, yank her to her feet and drag her out of the place. But he had too much at stake not to play it smart. The club seemed to be smothering him. Somehow he had to get out. He tried to keep his voice unruffled. "I got a headache, kid. A real big one. I need a sniff of air."

She was immediately contrite. He kissed her upturned mouth and drew her up almost gently, his hand caressing her back, stroking the cool skin of her throat, her loose hair. In the hazy light, her face seemed to glow. Buzz felt a sense of power growing within him. Whenever he wanted to, he could play it just right. Yeah, he really had a way with dames, and Diane was a real nifty little trick. Too good to hand over to Nucci. He almost wished he could play it straight. He and Diane could do things for each other. But he'd better forget the romantic mush. He had to keep his mind on the ball. It had to bounce his way tonight.

Outside, he linked his arm in hers. They walked side by side, their bodies touching. They didn't speak until they reached the corner. He swung her around to him, hugging her, smiling down at her.

She asked, "Where are we going, Buzz?"

"I dunno. I been thinkin' maybe we could drop into my pad and play a few records."

She didn't meet his eyes. She knew the score all right, what was expected of her. He could see it in the little curl of her lip. He could see something else too. She'd been putting on an act all night. Underneath she was scared. Now that the heat was on, she'd chicken out if she could. That was something he didn't dare let happen.

She said softly, "Buzz, I'm getting tired. Take me home."

It was time to get sore now, to put on the injured act. He dropped his arms to his side and stared down at her. Then he shrugged. "Sure, I'll put you in a cab. I guess I won't be seeing you no more. I guess we're washed up."

"Oh, Buzz, I didn't mean that."

Deliberately he made his voice harsh. "Then what did you mean? You think I'm trying to pull something on you? Ain't that what you think?"

"No, Buzz. It's just that it's late and you said you had a headache."

"To hell with it. I been playing this straight. Ain't I been showing you respect?"

"Oh, Buzz."

"So now I'm getting low on the dough and I reckoned we could make things cozy at my joint, play us a couple of records and drink some beer. But that ain't good enough for a fancy frill like you. You got it all pegged that I'm a guy on the make. That's okay by me, sugar. As far as I'm concerned, you've had it."

He spun away from her and started striding along, his heels loud on the concrete. For a dozen steps there was silence behind him and he almost thought he'd called the play wrong. Then her footsteps clattered on the sidewalk and she was calling his name. He walked on but he slowed his pace a little, letting her catch up with him. She clasped his arm but he jerked it away. Then she was in front of him, pleading.

It was hard not to laugh because the dumb chick read the lines just as if he'd written them for her.

Pretty soon it was he who was saying to forget it all, that they'd play the platters some other time and she who was insisting that they go to his pad. She was crying and he leaned down and took her in his arms, molded her body close against him. He really let himself go then, kissing the tears from her eyes, making with the sweet talk, telling her how crazy he was about her. Yeah, he let out the valves and she was lapping it up just like any two-bit grind.

A cab came cruising along and slid up to the curb. The cat at the wheel gave them a curious look but Buzz waved him on. He had things under control and it felt good. He hoped Nucci was really working himself into a lather. The more of a dither the stud got in, the easier it would be to catch him off base. And that was important. A shank artist like Nucci could be dangerous even when you had a rod in your hand.

It wasn't far from the Moontime Club to his pad. Only ten blocks or so. In the end they decided to walk it. Buzz was glad. It would give him a chance to case the hive where he lived. He had to have privacy to spring this deal. Somebody sniffing around could really queer his pitch. If there were too many lights on, he'd try to stall for a while, suggesting that they get something to eat first or go for a beer.

But when they turned into the block, he could see the building was dark. The only light on was in the first floor front where Belle Foley lived. Foley was a real geek, a dame who hit the bottle hard. Buzz didn't need to worry about her. Even if she heard a shot or a scream, if she tried to get up she'd probably fall on her face.

The rest of the block was quiet too, not a soul in sight except an old guy walking his dog at the far end. Buzz stopped at the outer door. He took Diane's hand in his. "Look, sugar, you got any doubts about Buzz Baxter's intentions, you just say the word and we'll forget all about it."

She didn't answer but pushed by him into the dimly lit hallway. Now that the thing was so close, he had the jitters again. He almost wished she'd deuced out on him. Up to now he'd been too preoccupied with getting her here to think about anything else. But in a couple of minutes he'd be up against Nucci. And Nucci wasn't any half-baked punk. He was a real killer. Buzz couldn't afford a single slip because if he did, he'd be the guy who was pushing up daisies.

His mouth felt dry and he ran his tongue over his lips. Upstairs Foley's radio was booming away. That was very good. It would cover up any noise that they might make.

He'd been holding back and he saw that Diane was watching him curiously. She touched his hand. "What's the matter, Buzz?"

"Nothing. Come on."

He led her down the hall. He fumbled around with his key, pretending to unlock the door, even though he knew that Nucci would leave the catch off. He made plenty of noise, just in case Nucci had got tired of the closet and come out to stretch, he'd have time to take cover.

When the door opened, the room was in darkness. He put in his hand and clicked on the switch. The light flooded out into the hall. He watched Diane enter the room but he hung back, feeling a prickle of fear in his fingertips, a tight knot in his stomach.

This was it, he thought. The real thing. He was breathing hard and he couldn't seem to force himself to pass through the door.

Then Diane screamed. Buzz stood frozen where he was. What the hell was happening? Had Nucci showed himself already?

Diane screamed again. Buzz managed to draw the gun from his windbreaker pocket and lurched over the threshold.

## 15

The closet door was wide open and Buzz could see its gaping emptiness. He whirled around, trying to find Nucci, fearful of being taken by surprise, almost feeling the rip of Nucci's knife. But Nucci was nowhere in the room and there was no possible hiding place except the closet. He turned to Diane, caught a glimpse of her white face and staring eyes. Her lips opened and her throat contracted to scream for the third time. He clamped his hand across her mouth, stifling the noise. But his eyes followed the direction of her pointing finger.

A figure was lying on the bed, half covered by a sheet. Not Nucci, but a girl. She was lying flat on her back, one bare breast showing, an arm dangling over the edge of the bed so that the fingers touched the floor. The head was twisted sideways, the features concealed by the pillow, so that only a tangle of blonde hair showed.

Buzz took two uncertain steps toward the bed. There was a dark stain on the upper part of the breast. Blood. It had to be blood. It had formed a rivulet across the shoulder and onto the sheet. Buzz moved closer. He knew who the girl was—Dottie Marr. He stared down at her. There was more blood on the sheet, lower down. He forced himself to touch her, turn her head. Her eyes were round, glassy, vacant; her tongue protruded from between her teeth.

She was dead. There was nothing he could do for her even if he wanted to. But he wasn't thinking of Dottie. He was thinking of the trap that was closing in on him. Dottie was dead in his bed and no one to swear that it was not he who had killed her.

He twitched the sheet back, saw the long ragged wounds across the abdomen, beneath the breasts. Nucci. But how could he prove it?

He stood still, fighting the panic that sent nausea through his body. How could he have been so stupid as to have forgotten about Dottie? He could visualize the scene. Dottie creeping into the apartment, probably half stoned, lighting a reefer, beginning to undress. Maybe she had left the room dark, the way she often did when Buzz was asleep. And Nucci, watching her from the crack of the closet door. Waiting until she was close or until her back was turned. Then stepping out, seizing her, choking her cries with his thick, strong fingers. He must have thrown her on the bed and then when he was finished with her slashed his knife deep into her body again and again.

Maybe Nucci had thought she was Diane at first. Maybe he'd felt cheated and revenged himself by the thrusts of his knife. But how could you tell what a psycho like Nucci would think?

Dottie, the little fool! He'd thought after the beating two nights before, after the way she'd left him the next morning, that she wouldn't be around, not for a while at least. But she had had to come back, ruining his plans. Anger burned inside him, not against Nucci but against Dottie. How many times did he have to kick the little bitch out to make it stick? He was almost glad that Nucci had killed her, except for the spot it put him in.

A strangled sob behind him jerked him around. Diane had collapsed in the chair by the table and buried her head in her hands. His anger turned to Diane. The dead girl in the bed could wait. Diane was the immediate danger. He saw the knife close to the table. He knelt, picked it up and held it in his hand. For one frantic moment he thought of plunging it into Diane. It was the only way he could be sure of her silence.

But that wasn't using his noodle. He couldn't panic. If he went haywire now, he was going to land right in the chair. The shock of the realization sent a tingling through his body, made him want to cry, to run. But somehow he'd have to pull himself together. He'd done it last night in Gladys Maintree's apartment; he could do it again. The gauge was the stuff to pull him through. It always had when he reached a crisis. The only reefer he'd smoked tonight was the one he'd shared with Diane. Another one wouldn't do him any harm. But he'd have to be careful.

He lit the reefer with shaking fingers and dragged the smoke in greedily, feeling the power flood back into him. By the time Diane raised her head he knew what he had to do. She was Willis Griscom's daughter, wasn't she? If he used her right, she'd be his protection, his safeguard. She'd have to be pulled in, pulled in deep, so that no one could touch Buzz Baxter without involving Diane.

He went to her quickly, pressed her face up against his chest as though shielding her from sight of the body. He said softly, "Diane. Diane, honey. It's Dottie Marr. She's dead. Nucci's killed her."

She looked up at him, her face drained of blood, her eyes still wet. "What are we going to do, Buzz?"

He made his voice harsh. "You better tear right out of here and grab a cab. You better forget you ever heard of a guy called Buzz Baxter."

Her eyes widened a little and her chin set in a stubborn line. He'd played the right angle, Buzz knew. The noble gesture had been the payoff. She'd stick with him now.

"Buzz, I can't just leave you."

"You've got to, sugar. This is trouble with a capital T."

"What'll you do if I go?"

He hesitated, not quite sure of her reaction. "Call the cops I guess. What else?"

"But Buzz—"

"Yeah?"

"Supposing they think you killed her?"

He let out his breath. She'd swallowed the bait, said just what he'd wanted her to say. He let his voice go bitter. "That's exactly what they're going to think. They're going to drag Buzz Baxter down to the jailhouse and throw the keys away."

"They can't. I was with you all night. I can prove it. There are the people at the Moontime Club too."

"You been with me from ten on. We don't know when Dottie was killed. We don't know nothin' except she's dead. Anyway—" He let the phrase drop, spreading his hands.

"What are you trying to tell me, Buzz?"

"Just this. I ain't got a chance. I told you once I got a record. Sure, it was meatball rap when I was a kid, but the cops don't forget. Once a con, always a criminal. That's the way they reckon. You think they're going to swallow a line about Nucci coming in here and polishing off Dottie? Not while they got their hands on Buzz Baxter. That's for sure. They'll want a confession and they'll get it."

"How can they, Buzz, when it's Nucci who killed her?"

"Maybe you don't believe the stuff about the rubber hose, the billiard cues, the lights in your eyes. But I been through it. I ain't no hero. If the cops want a confession out of me, they'll get it. There's only so much a guy can take."

"If I stay with you, they'll have to listen to me."

"You got any idea what that means? Newspaper stories. Headlines. Front-page stuff. Willis Griscom's daughter—"

"If we can find Nucci, maybe we can make him confess."

"You're having pipe dreams, sugar. As far as the cops are concerned, Nucci's the little guy who ain't there. We tell a story about him threatening you and how he's been hounding me. What happens? The cops give us a great big laugh. Dottie's dead right here in my pad. It ain't going to take the cops long to learn about me and you. They put two and two together and they'll add it up just one way. It's a triangle. I'm on the make for you and Dottie's in the way so I stick a knife into her."

"Why did Dottie come here, Buzz?"

"How do I know? She was a girl on the loose, with only one idea in her head: how to feed her habit. Maybe she came to knock me up for a couple bucks. Maybe she was so stoned she didn't know what she was doing."

"There's some way out. There's got to be."

That was what he wanted her to say. But he still had to be careful. He couldn't tell how far she'd string along. He looked down at her, making himself speak slowly. "Yeah, there's a way. Just one way, Diane. It's risky, but it's the only chance to keep in the clear for both you and me. Once I go to the cops, they're going to trace my movements. They're going to learn you were with me tonight and they're going to smear you, sugar. And there's another thing. Supposing in the end we pin the kill on Nucci. Why do you think he was on my tail? Because I'd taken over his route delivering junk. Do you know what they do to you when they catch you pushing? It's ten to fifteen years. Baby, before I call the cops we might as well kiss each other goodbye because we ain't going to be together no more, not for a long, long time. Maybe never again."

"Oh, Buzz."

"I didn't kill her, Diane, and as of last night, I'm through with pushing. I got a right to try to beat the rap, haven't I? If you'll help me I can do it. I'm going to get Dottie out of here, far, far away, to a place where nothing points to Buzz Baxter."

"I'll help you, Buzz. I'll do anything you say."

He grinned, feeling good in spite of everything. "Fix your make-up, sugar, and get a grip on yourself. I'm taking you down to the all-night café on the corner. I'm going to leave you there for half an hour or so. You got to act like nothing's wrong. That you're just waitin' for a heavy date. Think you can do it, Diane?"

"Of course I can. But shouldn't I be here with you?"

He shook his head. "You can help most by doing just what I say."

"All right, Buzz."

"Solid, sugar." He held her tight for a minute, kissing her. Then he led her over to the cracked mirror above the washstand. He stood between her and the bed while she touched up her lipstick, brushed her face with powder. When she turned she managed a wan smile. If you looked close, you could still tell she'd been crying, but what the hell, there were lots of reasons for a dame weeping. Buzz took her arm and got her out quick. He didn't take her clear to the café but stopped just short of the pool of light spilled by the plate-glass window. He started to kiss her, then changed his mind. Some snooper might notice them smooching on the street. Right now the less attention they attracted the better. He whispered, "Make it good, baby."

She kept on walking, holding herself erect, her head high. She went through the revolving door without looking back.

Buzz turned and started walking slowly toward his room. If he was going to get Dottie out of his pad, the first thing he needed was a car. Renting one was too dangerous and trying to steal one was taking a double risk. Besides he didn't have a jumper and didn't know how to use one even if he did. Looking around for a car he could grab might take hours, and he didn't have that kind of time. But there was one person who could help him. That was Belle Foley. The old bag had a beat-up Ford stashed away in the mews, right where it was handy. All he had to do was get his hands on the keys and he'd be right in clover.

Up till now he'd always tried to steer clear of Foley. The fat dame was a real lush. She was always hanging around the stairs asking him if he didn't want to come up for a little drinkie-winkie. He'd always turned her down. All she spelled was trouble on wheels. Anyway he never went for the juice. He was strictly a reefer boy.

But tonight was different. He could use Belle Foley. By the way her radio was banging it out, she probably had a few drinks tucked under her belt already. He'd seen her that way plenty of times and she'd always given him the wink. Getting close to Belle Foley ought to be easy. When she was in the mood she'd sell her eyebrows for a little loving up or a bottle of gin.

A bottle of gin! He snapped his fingers. Why hadn't he thought of that before? It was a lot faster than making with the sweet talk. He remembered that there was a liquor store across the street from the restaurant where he'd left Diane. He retraced his steps and crossed the street. He picked out a fifth of Gordon's and told the clerk to wrap it up. With the bottle under his arm, he didn't need to worry about his reception. Belle would welcome him like a millionaire uncle with one foot in the grave.

As soon as he pushed open the outer door of the house, the blast of her radio nearly deafened him. It didn't mean anything. Sometimes she'd pass out and leave the radio running all night. He hoped her door wasn't locked. If he had to knock, he might wake up the nosy old guy across the hall.

He took the stairs quietly and listened outside Belle's door. He could hear her stumbling around. He tried the door but it didn't give under his fingers, so he tapped lightly. He heard her yell, "Go to hell. Lea' me alone." But all the same she came lumbering to the door and threw it open. She swayed against the jamb, her eyes beady. "If you come to squawk about the radio, you can go soak your head. A girl's got to have a little fun, ain't she?"

He managed a grin. "Who's squawking?"

She squinted at him. "Oh, it's you, Buzz. I thought it was that old buzzard across the hall, pestering me again. Come on in."

He followed her into the room, looking at the faded blue kimono that clung to her broad buttocks, her scuffed felt slippers. She picked up a bottle with a finger of gin in it. She said, "There ain't much left, but I guess there's a snifter."

He laughed and started stripping the paper off the bottle he'd brought. "You needn't worry. I brought reinforcements."

She said, "My baby," and threw her arms about him, almost knocking the bottle to the floor. He winced at the smell of her sour breath and the touch of her flabby breasts but he fought down his revulsion. This wasn't any time to be finicky. She swayed away from him. "You wouldn't be conning me, would ya? Nobody gives Mamma Belle nothing less they got a proposition."

"I was in the mood for a drink, is all. I don't like to drink alone."

She waved her hand in a gesture that almost sent her sprawling. "Okay. You mix 'em."

There were tins of grapefruit juice on the table. He kept his back to her as he mixed the drinks. He spiked hers heavily, making it three-quarters gin. For himself he poured straight fruit juice.

When he turned, she was seated on the bed, propped up by the pillows. She patted the crumpled sheet beside her. She said, "Mamma's wise to you, Buzz. But you needn't worry. Mamma likes you."

Did she really think he'd come up to make a pass at her? He'd like to throw the drink right in that old witch's puss of hers. But that could wait. Tonight he wasn't in any position to call the signals. He sat down beside her, handed her the glass. She gulped at the drink, slopping part of it down her kimono. She leaned back, gasping, letting the kimono slip down across her heavy breasts. The spilled drink started to spread across the sheet. He took the glass out of her hand, set it on the bedside table.

She opened her eyes. "What you waiting for, Buzz?"

"I want to get pixied first. Come on, finish up your drink and I'll mix another."

She reached for the glass, drank most of what remained. He took it from her and went back to the table. When he returned her eyes were closed and she was breathing stertorously. He placed the drink beside her. He moved quietly to the bureau where he'd seen her purse. He opened it and found the keys. When he looked up, her eyes were open, watching him. He crossed to her, stood above her, waiting. She struggled up on one elbow, but then collapsed. He waited for a minute longer but she didn't move. She wasn't going to make any trouble for him, not tonight anyway. And in the state she was in, she'd probably forget he'd ever been here by tomorrow.

He was all set now, but he'd have to work fast. He tiptoed across the room and out into the hall, pulling the door shut silently behind him.

As soon as he was back in his room, he went to work. The old army blankets he'd bought in a second-hand store had cleaner's marks on them. He sliced them out with his switchblade. He spread the blankets on the floor beside the bed. He eased the girl's body off the bed, so that she sprawled on the blankets. The body had begun to stiffen, but he was able to pull in the arms, draw up the legs.

He examined the bloody sheets, found laundry marks and cut them away. He almost missed a second set of marks at the foot of one of the sheets. He swore under his breath. Mistakes like this could trip him up, send him to the chair. It was better to take a few extra minutes and be sure of what he was doing. He balled up the sheets, placed them beside the girl and folded the blankets across her in a crude bundle.

He straightened up, lit a reefer and looked around. Blood had soaked onto the straw mattress and there was a stain on the floor. Dottie's clothing lay at the foot of the bed, the high-heeled shoes were kicked under it. Should he clean up now or wait until he'd got rid of Dottie? He weighed the risks involved. You could explain blood and a girl's clothing if you had to, but you couldn't explain away a corpse.

A sudden thought struck him. What if Nucci had laid a trap for him and called the cops? If he were caught in the act of moving Dottie's body, he'd be a dead duck for sure. All the same he took time out to turn the mattress, toss Dottie's clothing into the closet and pull a rug over the stain. There wasn't much chance anyone would drop in on him this late, but you never could tell.

The back door leading to the mews was kept bolted from the inside. Buzz tried to draw them back gently but they were rusted and at first they wouldn't budge. He had to put a lot of pressure on, and then they slid back with a screech and the door banged open. The crash made Buzz's nerves jump and the tremors in his hands started again. He went to the foot of the stairs and listened but no one seemed to have been awakened by the noise.

The driveway in the mews was cindered. In spite of Buzz's precautions, his feet made crackling sounds. Belle's car wasn't locked. He climbed inside and fitted the key into the ignition. The motor growled but refused to catch. It took half a dozen tries before it coughed into life. Then it caught with a sudden deafening roar. Buzz backed the car up to the door. He was sweating all over. It seemed as though he'd made enough noise to raise the dead, but no lights had gone on in the windows. He peered up at the black panes, trying to see if anyone was behind them, watching him. There was no sign of life anywhere.

He was back in the hall with his hand on the knob of his door when he heard the creek of the stairs and then the sound of clumsy footsteps. He stood where he was, his back turned, too frightened to move. A slurred voice said, "Buzz, baby, why'd you leave me? Mamma needs you."

Belle Foley. The old bag had chased down after him. His fists clenched and anger replaced his fear. He whirled around. She was clinging to the railing, squinting down at him, her face a grotesque, grinning mask. If she should notice the open door at the rear, her own car just beyond it, she'd raise a row that would wake the whole house.

He had to reach her fast, get her back to her room before she spotted anything wrong. He took the stairs two at a time. He wanted to smash her face in, push her down the rest of the flight. But he'd have to keep hold of himself. If he blew his top he'd be signing his own death warrant.

He took her by the arm and she leaned her weight

on him, giggling. "Were you trying to walk out on Mamma, Buzz?"

His fingers dug into her arm but she was too juiced-up to notice. Getting her up the stairs was a job. She stopped at every step, raising her flabby face to be kissed, babbling baby talk. The stairs took almost ten minutes and when he finally got her as far as the corridor his patience snapped. He almost dragged her to her room.

She wouldn't let go of him. Her fingers twined in the buttonholes of his windbreaker. He didn't dare jerk away and leave her. She'd follow him back into the hall, watch while he carried Dottie's body to the car.

She was tugging at him, leading him toward the bed. He let himself be led for a few steps. Then he fell behind and placed the flat of his palm between her shoulders. She started to turn, giggling in protest. He didn't give her a chance. His foot shot out, catching her ankle. At the same time he pushed, using all the pent-up, angry force within him. She gave a squeal of terror as she plunged forward. She sprawled to the floor with a jar that shook the room and her head struck the heavy curved leg of the bed, making a thick, pulpy sound. One leg jerked spasmodically, then she rolled over flat on her face.

He looked down at her, fighting the impulse to drive his foot into her prone body. She didn't move. The faded kimono rucked up high on her heavy thighs and her felt slippers had fallen off, leaving her feet bare. She might be hurt badly, but there wasn't time to see. He made for the hall stairs and raced down them. The only thing that mattered now was getting Dottie away from the house.

He flung the door of his room open. He managed to lift the blankets containing Dottie's body to his shoulder. He staggered out into the hall. He didn't look to see if he was observed. He didn't care any longer. He stuffed his burden into the back of the car.

When he straightened up he was shaking all over. He clutched at the car, holding himself up. Then he turned slowly, glaring back into the lighted hall. No one was there. No sound. But somehow he couldn't believe that he was alone. There had to be someone in the shadows, watching him, spying on him.

Suddenly his control snapped. He yelled, "Come out. Come on out, you bastards."

His voice echoed through the mews. From an open window up above, a voice answered, "Shut up, you drunken fool. Go to bed."

Buzz stared about him, unable to locate the window from which the voice had come. Then suddenly he wanted to laugh. He tried to choke back the hysterical spasms of laughter that gurgled in his throat. He bent double with the effort but the laughter came ripping out in a thin neighing squeal. He was still laughing when he crawled in behind the wheel.

## 16

For Diane the lights of the cafeteria had a wavering, unnatural brilliance and her own voice seemed to come from far away as she ordered a sandwich and coffee. When the tray was pushed toward her, she carried it to a corner table. Her body seemed detached, without feeling. She looked at her hands and was surprised by their steadiness. She took a sip of the coffee. It was so hot that it burned her tongue, but it was devoid of taste.

This was a nightmare, and soon Buzz would come to wake her up, to laugh at her, to reassure her. The cafeteria was nearly empty and the few people who were at the tables ate in a preoccupied silence that added to the air of unreality. Diane shivered and twisted her face toward the wall.

She shut her eyes, trying to free herself of the image of Dottie Marr's nearly naked body, the rumpled, bloodstained sheets. She had gone to Buzz's room tonight with her eyes open, knowing what he expected of her, planning to submit. She knew that he had lied to her when he said he had no money. She had seen the roll of bills in his wallet. But she hadn't cared about that. Tonight was to have marked the end of flight. In union with Buzz she had expected to dispel her own sense of aloneness, of drifting. Instead she had encountered murder. Now there was no release from flight, only a quickened tempo.

She grasped the edge of the table until her hands went numb. The numbness spread upward into her body and mind. She didn't know how long she sat motionless, but when she took another sip of the coffee she was surprised that it had grown cold.

Where was Buzz? Why was, he taking so long? She looked about the restaurant and scanned the street. There was no sign of him. She saw the counterman watching her curiously and she forced herself to sit down again, to wait quietly. But now that the questions had started in her mind, there seemed no end to them. What had Dottie Marr been doing in Buzz's place? Buzz had said that Dottie had come for money. But could she believe him? Buzz had kept his address secret from her, but Dottie had known it. Dottie must have come there, gotten in somehow, undressed. Had Buzz and Dottie been living together? What did it matter? She had known Buzz was no angel. With a man like Buzz there must have been plenty of girls.

Why had Buzz been so sure that it was Nucci who had killed Dottie? He'd spoken Nucci's name at once. It was almost as though he'd been expecting Nucci to be there. But, after all, wasn't Nucci the natural suspect? He'd threatened to kill Buzz, and threatened Diane, too. But if Nucci had been waiting in Buzz's room and Buzz had known, what did that mean? Could Buzz have been taking her to Nucci? Had she, not Dottie, been the intended victim tonight? But that was crazy. She wouldn't permit herself to think things like that. She could believe almost anything of Buzz, but not that he'd hand her over to Nucci.

A new idea came to her. Could Buzz have killed Dottie after all? Could he have known that the girl was lying on his bed all through the long evening they'd spent together? She swept the thought aside. Buzz might be capable of murder. She'd seen the violence in him, heard it in his music. But Buzz would panic afterward, seek safety in flight.

The knife was Nucci's weapon. There was no reason to suspect anyone but him. But once Buzz moved the body, who would believe his story—or her own? Maybe she should go back, try to persuade Buzz to notify the police. No, it wouldn't do any good. By now it was too late.

She stirred restlessly. A shadow fell across the white-tiled table. She looked up, her lips ready to shape Buzz's name. A harsh voice said, "Hello, sweetheart. You waitin' for Buzz?"

The grating tones struck terror into her even before she recognized Nucci's pale, narrow face. She couldn't have answered if she'd wanted to. She looked around for help, but the only people anywhere near were a young couple who leaned close together whispering to each other. Even if they wanted to help her, what could they do against a man like Nucci?

Nucci lowered himself in the chair opposite her. He spoke in a husky whisper, "I ain't been far away, sweetheart. I been hanging around, seeing what you and Buzz would do."

"What do you want?"

"Keep your hair on, sister. I'm here to do you a favor. So far Buzz is bein' a good boy. He ain't called the cops nor done nothin' silly like that. But maybe you been getting some ideas sittin' here waiting for him. So let me tell you something. Once the nabs grab hold of Frank Nucci, it's going to be curtains for Buzz Baxter." His grin became wider. "It's this way, baby. A guy like me sort of gets used to the idea that someday maybe he'll take the hot squat. But with a punk like Baxter it's different. He'd be screaming every step of the way. And believe me, if I go, I'm taking Buzz with me. Watchin' him squirm would be almost worth the price of the ticket."

"You killed Dottie Marr."

"I ain't sayin' yes, I ain't sayin' no. But Buzz shouldn't have double-crossed me tonight. Well, I'll be ankling. You just tell Buzz for me that he better make things good. There ain't a thing to link me to Dottie. Not a thing. And it better stay that way, because I know just how to fit the straps around Buzz."

Nucci's lean body rose and towered above her. "Just one more little item and I'll be on my way. In case you're thinkin' of tossing Buzz to the wolves, you better think again. Because you ain't in the clear, not by a long shot. If they fry Buzz and me, they're going to get you as an accessory. They wouldn't burn you, baby, but it can get mighty lonely in the slammer. Yeah, them cells can really get you down. So be a good girl, sister, because it's a long time between bangs when them prison gates slam behind you."

She edged her chair away from him. She wanted to scream, but she willed herself to remain silent. A scene now could mean the end of everything. She mustn't give way to hysteria.

He moved off. She looked up just in time to see his elongated shadow strike across the window. Where was he going? To track down Buzz? To threaten Buzz as he had just threatened her?

Until Nucci had warned her, she'd not thought of any danger to herself. Only to Buzz. But now she envisioned the newspaper headlines, the trial. If she escaped, ran to the police, she'd be safe from prison. She'd committed no crime. But Nucci would have a score to settle with her—and so would Buzz. And who would help her? Not her weak, ineffectual mother. Maybe her father. But already she could feel the whiplash of his anger, her stepmother's scorn. She had sought freedom in Buzz; now, if she were not careful, she'd lose freedom forever. Buzz was her only hope. She couldn't wait any longer. She had to find him, be with him, make sure he didn't fumble.

She got up unsteadily, crossed to the counter and paid her check. A thin drizzle of rain had started, making the empty street glisten blackly. She hesitated on the corner. The cross street where Buzz lived seemed darker than ever, filled with furtive silent movement. The rain made soft hollow sounds as it fell on the litter of paper at the curb. The block stretched out interminably. Somewhere among the shadows she was sure that Nucci was watching.

She began to run, quietly at first, then in frantic haste. A light struck across her face, blinding her. It was like a gigantic spotlight, following her, stripping her naked with its brilliant glare. She cowered against a building, shielding her face with her arm, not realizing at first that the glare came from the headlights of a car.

She heard her name called. "Diane. Diane. For God's sake, what you doing?"

It was Buzz calling her. She could see the car now, its door open. She ran to it and jumped in.

"Buzz, Nucci was in the café. He's around somewhere."

"Yeah, I know. I caught him in my headlights just before I saw you."

"He says—"

"Stow it. We gotta get out of here fast."

Tight lines showed in his face, and fear made his voice high-pitched. Somehow the knowledge that he was frightened, too, steadied her. She slumped back against the seat, silent, watching him.

He drove erratically, skidding around the corners, crashing through a red light.

"You can't drive like this, Buzz. You'll be arrested."

"Shut up."

At Madison, he crowded a car to the curb. There was a shrill squeal of brakes. Buzz drove on, but the other car came after him, drew even. The driver leaned out of the window, shouting obscenities, then cut sharply across Buzz's path. Buzz jerked at the wheel.

The Ford bucked as it hit the curbing and jolted onto the sidewalk. Buzz braked just in time to avoid crashing into a building. He sat at the wheel, shaking uncontrollably. The other car drove on and the sound of laughter drifted back.

"Let me drive, Buzz. Please."

He didn't answer, but when she got out and circled the car he slid over. The grip of her hands on the wheel, the need to concentrate on driving helped her. There was no room in her mind for anything but the flickering green and red lights, the glistening road and the traffic that roared around her.

"Where shall we go?"

"I dunno. Over to the West Side Highway. Up along the river. We gotta find a quiet place."

"Is she—"

"Yeah. Dottie's in back."

The cold and the numbness crept over her again. Her hands gripped the wheel more tightly and she didn't dare turn to look at Buzz. Vaguely she was aware that they had come to Riverside Drive. She swung to the north and followed the murky gray ribbon of the Hudson.

Buzz said, "Tell me about Nucci."

She told him, keeping her voice brittle, not letting her eyes leave the road. She could hear his harsh breathing, sense the anger and violence within him as well as the frustration and the fear.

He said, "He can do what he says, take me to the chair with him. He's mean enough and crazy enough to try it."

"We can fight him, Buzz."

"How?"

"I don't know, but there's got to be a way."

They drove on in silence. The acrid smell of Buzz's reefer grew stifling. She took her hand from the wheel for a moment, pressed it on his. He drew away. She started to speak but he interrupted her irritably. "I'm trying to reckon out how to play my cards, baby. So leave me alone and button up. I got some heavy thinking to do."

The toll gate loomed ahead, a patch of uneven light in the thickening fog. Her pulse quickened to the danger.

But the guard took her money with bored unconcern.

Buzz was slouched down in the seat. But when they were through the barrier, he said tightly, "Let's get off the highway, down by the river somewhere. Okay, turn off here."

The Ford swerved onto a macadam roadway, slid between rows of dark houses. They struck a crossroad and Buzz told her to turn again. There was another turn, and another, until she lost all sense of direction, following his commands automatically. Twice he told her to stop, then as headlights flooded the road behind them, he urged her on.

It seemed to her that she had been driving forever, with Buzz hunched beside her, silent except for his snapped commands. Finally he growled, "A public road's too risky. I don't dare carry Dottie far and unless we find a good place to hide her, someone's likely to spot her right away. What we gotta do is find some place private, like a big estate. We gotta find it fast, too, or we ain't going to get back to the city until it's light."

The river had come back into view. A narrow park, bordered by a stone wall, stretched toward the embankment. On the other side, big houses, set amid spacious lawns, were limned against the gray sky.

"Drive slow. We're going to find us a spot."

Their headlights picked out rows of hedges, elaborate entrances to driveways. A moment later, Buzz leaned toward her. "I seen a name back there, James B. Maitland. That's Senator Maitland. He won't be around."

"What about his family? The servants?"

"That's a chance we take. We can't keep circling around or sooner or later someone's going to spot us and give us the B. We gofta dump Dottie before that happens."

"Buzz?"

"Yeah."

"How well did you know Dottie?"

"For God's sake, this ain't no time to turn green-eyed on me."

"It's not that. I've been thinking that once Dottie's body is found it won't take long to trace her back to you if you've been close."

"I've fixed that up. She ain't got no clothes. I sliced off the laundry marks."

"They'll take pictures of her. Someone will remember seeing you together. Maybe we're making a mistake. We could go back, tell the police everything."

"Hey, are you blowin' your conk? Talking like that when Nucci's ready to ring the gong." He bent forward and she could see his face, white and strained in the glow from the dashboard. He switched off the ignition. "Listen, baby, from here on in, I'm taking over."

He opened the door and stepped out onto the roadway. His feet gritted on the asphalt as he passed around the front of the car and opened the door on her side. He said roughly, "Shove over, baby."

She relinquished the wheel and moved to the other side of the seat without protest. He switched off the lights and made a U-turn where the road widened. The Ford moved almost soundlessly over the wet asphalt and then there was a soft crunching sound as the tires struck the gravel drive that led to the Maitland house.

The driveway was forked, one arm leading to the portico of the house, the other winding through a copse. Diane watched the blank windows. No lights flicked on and there was no sign of life. Buzz picked the branch of the road that led away from the house. Trees lined the path, shrouded it in black shadows. The boughs of an evergreen, heavy with rain, scraped the top of the Ford.

They came to a clearing and Buzz backed in, wheeled the car so that it faced the road. He said softly, "This is it."

Diane didn't answer but looked straight ahead. She heard the sounds of the front door of the Ford opening, then the back, the slither of the weighted blanket brushing against the upholstery of the seat. The car swayed to one side a little, then righted itself with a jolt. Buzz grunted, swore softly.

Diane stared into the darkness, pressing the knuckles of her hand against her lips to keep back her rising nausea. Far ahead a tiny circle of light flickered, moved in an arc across the path. Someone was there, moving toward them, picking out the way with a flashlight.

"Buzz." Her whisper sounded loud in the silence of the night.

"For Christ's sake, keep quiet."

"Someone's coming."

She heard Buzz swear, then his figure filled the opening of the door. He squeezed in beside her. Down the roadway the circle of light swung upward, sending a tiny beam along the tunnel formed by the trees. The motor sputtered, then roared. The Ford lunged forward in the darkness. The flashlight seemed to rush toward them, to become glaringly bright. Buzz switched on his headlights. A man stood impaled in their brilliance. Diane caught only a glimpse of him. He was an old man with a fringe of white hair that showed beneath a cap with a broken visor. His face was pinched and thin. He blinked into the light, his stance awkward.

As the car came hurtling down upon him, he tried to throw himself to the side of the road. There was a high-pitched scream, but Diane was not sure whether it had come from her throat or that of the old man. There was a sickening thud as something struck hard against the fender.

"Buzz, stop. You've hit him."

There was no answer. The car gathered momentum, caromed from the driveway onto the asphalt road. Diane clutched at his arm. "He's hurt. We've got to help him."

"Cut it out, Diane. Can't you get it into your head this is a murder rap? We gotta get clear."

"You didn't need to strike him."

"What was I to do? Tell him we just dropped in to dump a body?"

"He may be injured badly."

"So what? If we stopped, he'd have a description of us. Even if we'd convinced him we'd just gone up the path for a little necking, he'd remember and when Dottie's body is found we'd be right on the dime. Besides, he might have smelled a rat, started poking around right away. As soon as he'd found Dottie, he'd have phoned the cops. We'd never get through the road traps they'd set up."

"I don't care. We've got to go back."

"Use your noodle, sugar. We go back there and we'll be nabbed sure as hell. It means the chair for me. And if you don't care about me, think about yourself. Like Nucci told you, you're an accessory. That means ten years in jail, maybe twenty. Does some old coot you don't even know mean that much to you?"

Diane remained motionless, pressing her back against the door, trying to see Buzz's face in the darkness. Dottie's death had frightened her, but it had had no meaning. It was a trap that Nucci had set and they had a right to clear themselves. But the old man was different. Buzz had struck him deliberately, without giving him a chance to jump clear.

She bit her lip but she couldn't hold back a whimper of fear. Buzz slowed the car. His voice beat at her, hard and savage, grating, almost like Nucci's. "Get this straight, Diane. We're in this together, me and you. You're mixed up in murder right up to your pretty neck. But we can beat the rap if we stick together."

"What do you want me to do?"

"That's the way to talk, baby. Just leave the thinking to me. First of all we're going to get married, so neither of us can be made to testify against the other. But there ain't time for that tonight and we gotta work fast. So tomorrow we see Willis Griscom and tell him we're already hitched. Your old man's got to help us or we'll pull him down with us. So I'm calling the shots."

"It won't work, Buzz. You don't know what my father's like."

"Yeah, well maybe there's some things you don't know about Griscom. He's front man for the syndicate. He's one guy who can really pull the cops off our backs. And he's gotta play ball because if this hits the papers, he's in a mess."

"You sound like Nucci, Buzz."

"Maybe that's good. Nucci's a smart cookie. He knows his way around. But he ain't going to outsmart me because I'm going to have Griscom on my side."

"You can't stand up against my father, Buzz. You're crazy if you think you can. "

He swung the car to the side of the road with a savage twist of the wheel and braked to a jolting stop. He jerked about on the seat to face Diane. She twisted from him. His fingers bit into her shoulder as he swung her toward him, and his eyes blazed with anger.

"What's the matter with you, baby? I tell you we're getting hitched and you act like I was asking you to a funeral. Maybe you think I don't know the score. Maybe you think I ain't hip to a guy like Griscom. Let me tell you something—either you take me to him or I pull it myself. I tell ya I got him by the short hairs and all I'm askin' is that he takes me off the dime for a kill I didn't do. So make up your mind, baby. Are you with me or are on the other side?"

She straightened up and he could feel the muscles of her arm grow taut. Her voice was thin. "All right, Buzz, I'll take you to him. I'm meeting him tomorrow at four o'clock in the lounge of the Piermont. You can meet me there a few minutes earlier. But it's not going to do any good."

He fought back the angry words that sprang to his lips. "Look, Diane, we're both ready to flip. But we can't afford to rumble. We gotta get close. Maybe I been going about this wrong but I'm really gone on you. I been wantin' to marry you all the time. But I knew we wasn't in the same class so I zipped my lip. Now things are different."

She said wearily, "Yes, they're different."

He drew her close but her body remained taut and when he tried to kiss her she turned her face away.

"What's eatin' you, baby? I'm Buzz. Remember me?"

"Please, Buzz, we've got to get back. It will be light soon. If a police car comes along they'll stop and ask questions."

For a moment he remained undecided. Then his hands went back to the wheel and he eased the car into the roadway. At an intersection, he glanced toward her. She did not return his look but remained motionless, staring ahead of her through the rain-splotched windshield.

# 17

Unfamiliar sounds echoed in the hallway. The clamor of heavy boots on the stairs. Loud voices. Buzz forced himself into wakefulness and lay listening. Cops. When you'd done a stretch in the slammer, when you'd worn out your ankles around Times Square, you could smell 'em even through closed doors.

He slid off the bed, tiptoed to the door, opened it a crack and peered out. He hadn't been mistaken. It was the cops all right. He could see the blue-clad shoulder of a nab leaning against the balustrade. Upstairs there was a babble of voices and more foot beats. He'd been holding his breath. Now he let it out sharply. With the cops around he'd have to be on the ball. Wipe the cobwebs out of his brain.

Why were the cops upstairs? Belle Foley, of course. In the pressure of other things he'd almost forgotten her. Maybe she'd rung up the station, told a story about him tripping her. But he'd thought she'd been too high to know what the score was. Maybe she'd reported her car stolen. Well, it was back in the mews now with the keys in the ignition lock. She'd have a hard time making any story about him stick, especially when everyone knew how she lapped up the juice.

When the fuzz was around, the smart thing to do was pull out, pick yourself another piece of turf. But he couldn't get past the cop in the hall without being seen, and the window was too risky. He'd better sweat it out, find out how the ball was bouncing.

He'd slept in his clothes. He'd been too bushed when he got in this morning to care whether school kept or not. All he had wanted was to grab himself some kip. As soon as he'd hit the sack his eyes had closed. It hadn't occurred to him that the fuzz would be around so soon, but now he remembered the bloodstained mattress, the roll of Dottie's clothing in the closet. If the cops patted down the place, he'd have a lot of explaining to do. But maybe he was getting the wind up over nothing. If Foley had put in a squeal, why hadn't the cops come straight to his room, instead of tramping all over the place. Just the same, he'd better take precautions. He dug out an old spread from the bottom drawer of his bureau and tossed it over the bed. Then he gathered up some soiled shirts, took them to the closet and flung them down on top of Dottie's clothing.

He'd just finished when knuckles pounded on his door. Act natural, he warned himself. He crossed to the door, opened it wide. A lone policeman stood there. Buzz felt a little better. Cops always made their pinches in pairs.

"Yeah. What is it?" He was looking the cop over. A young fellow, big, with a pinkish, boy's face that had a scrubbed look. A real ox, Buzz thought; probably a rookie.

"Just checking," the cop said. "There's been an accident upstairs. Woman by the name of Belle Foley. Did you know her?"

"I seen her around, even blew the breeze with her a couple times. She hurt bad?"

"Bad enough for the morgue. They got her down there now."

Buzz's knees went weak and sickness crawled along his stomach. It hadn't occurred to him that Belle was dead. He'd thought she'd come out of it with a headache, with a concussion at the worst. If the cops caught wise to what had happened, they'd pin him to the wall. A manslaughter rap. Maybe murder, if they ever learned about his taking the car.

He backed into the room, let himself down on the chair by the table. The cop followed him. "It's hitting you hard."

"Yeah. I was jaw-blocking with her in the hall only yesterday."

"That's the way it goes. What time was it when you talked to her?"

Buzz felt confused, trapped. He'd only made the remark about Foley to cover his agitation. He should have kept his lip zipped. Now he'd have to start lying. "I dunno. Maybe three. Maybe four."

"Had she been drinking?"

"She always carried a load. Yeah, she was spiffed.

Hey, what happened to her?"

"We're not sure yet. Looks like she took a spill, cracked her head on the bed. It's queer, though. Usually a drunk just folds up. You didn't go up to her room with her, did you?"

There was no time to think. He had to answer fast. He shook his head.

"What about later? Did you see her again?"

"No."

"Hear any noises?"

"Just her radio. She always played it wide open."

"That's how she happened to he found. The old gent across the hall went to complain. When he knocked on her door, it opened. He saw her lying there and called the station. Do you know the old guy?"

"I seen him. I don't know his name."

"Mansey. He's quite a character. I hear he and Mrs. Foley had a couple of run-ins."

"I wouldn't know."

"We've been wondering if Mansey's story is on the up-and-up. There was somebody else in Foley's room last night. Two glasses on the table and a funny thing, one of them was plain grapefruit juice. Mansey doesn't drink."

"You said it was an accident." Buzz heard the shrillness of his own voice.

"Sure. But Foley went down hard. There could have been a fight. Mansey could have socked her."

Cold sweat was beading Buzz's forehead. He'd forgotten about the glass. Probably his fingerprints were all over it, around the room too. He should have said that he met Foley on the stairs last night, helped her to her room. That she'd been okay when he left her. Maybe he should change his story now, but it would arouse suspicion. As long as the cops thought it was an accident, they wouldn't dust for fingerprints. Probably this rookie was an eager beaver, trying to play Dick Tracy all on his own.

He'd been quiet too long. The cop was giving him the eye. He had to say something. Then he saw that the cop had turned, was looking at the roaches in the ashtray. He should have flushed them down the drain, but there were too many things to think of. He had to get rid of the cop somehow. If the nabs started searching, they'd turn up Dottie's clothes, the bloodstains, the revolver and switchblade in his windbreaker. Then they'd bust him for sure.

He got up. "I got an appointment. I gotta get cracking."

The cop took his time hauling out his notebook. "A few formalities. I'll have to have your name, where you work."

Buzz wanted to protest but he didn't dare. Finally the cop left. Buzz began to shake. He needed the boom bad. He lit up, but the stuff didn't send him. It might as well have been catnip for all the good it did. He had to get rid of the mattress and the clothing. But how could he do it with the fuzz all about? He grabbed a towel and scrubbed at the stain on the floor. But that just added another problem. Now he had to dump the towel somewhere.

How much time did he have? Not much, once they got to work on his fingerprints. His prints were on file, taken at the reformatory. He jerked upright, suddenly thinking of Belle Foley's car. His prints would be on it, and so would Diane's. He opened his window and looked out. The Ford was in the mews, right where he'd left it. But he didn't dare go out and start polishing it off. The cops would be sure to spot him. Besides, he only had an hour before he had to meet Diane and Willis Griscom.

Griscom was more important to him now than ever. He'd have to be on his toes, ready to pour on the oil or beat the guy down if he got tough. And here he was shaking like a witch. He swore at the cop, at Belle Foley. If the old bag hadn't been juiced up this wouldn't have happened. He'd be sailing in the clear with only Nucci to worry about.

He dressed carefully, working his way through a couple of reefers while he did so. He chose charcoal-gray slacks, a white-on-white shirt with a button-down collar, a string tie, the tweed jacket. He examined himself in the mirror. He looked sharp. His nerves were smoothing out too. Why had he been so jittery about Foley? If worst came to worst, he could admit he'd been in her room last night, that he'd borrowed her car. He'd say that she'd been plastered when he left her but that otherwise she'd been okay. They'd never prove he tripped her up, pushed her. How could you prove a thing like that?

He stood for a while admiring himself in the mirror.

What he saw made him feel good. He was a smooth-looking cat, a real hip guy, a boy on his way up. Griscom would see that. Griscom would give him a helping hand. He ground out his roach. He'd better not take any of the boom with him. Not while he was on the make with Griscom. He shoved the remaining sticks between some shirts. He thought of the revolver in his windbreaker pocket. If the cops should decide to pat down his pad, having a rod would look bad. All the same he couldn't afford to take it with him. The nosy nab outside might decide to search him.

He took the revolver out of the windbreaker and buried it beneath the crumpled papers in his wastebasket. He held the switchblade in his hand for a little while, then slid it into the side pocket of his jacket. Going out without a weapon of any kind always made him feel vulnerable. It was like hitting the street without your shoes on.

The cop was standing out on the stoop when he left, but he didn't seem to pay him any mind. Buzz walked along briskly without looking back. At the newsstand in front of the subway kiosk he bought a paper. He skimmed through it, even the back pages. Nothing about Dottie. Hell, when they found her body, they'd smear it all over the front page—Dottie would make headlines, after all. He folded up the paper, thrust it into his pocket and hailed a cruising cab. As he climbed in, he saw the cop had tagged along behind him, was only a few feet away. It gave Buzz a queasy feeling but he tried to shake it off. He'd need his wits about him when he talked to Griscom.

The Piermont was a real cushy joint. A doorman wearing half a ton of gold braid snapped the big door open. Inside, the place was all polished chrome and red leather, with a thick green carpet underfoot. When he'd grabbed himself a fistful of the Griscom dough, maybe he'd move into a dive like this, Buzz thought.

It didn't take him long to spot Diane. She was sitting on a banquette just inside the entrance. She was wearing a tailored suit of bottle green, sheer nylons, green pumps. Her blonde hair hung low on her shoulders. This place formed the right setting for her. She looked like the million-dollar baby that she was. Her face was cool, composed. You had to look twice before you saw the little pinched lines around her eyes, the pallor of her skin.

He went to her quickly, took her by both hands and pulled her to her feet. But she didn't come into his arms the way he'd expected. Instead she remained motionless, looking up at him, her face masklike in its stillness.

He said, "Act happy, sugar. Ain't everything rosy? Ain't me and you going to get hitched?"

"No, Buzz. I'm not going through with it."

"You ain't going through with it?" he repeated incredulously. "What do you mean? You deucin' out on me? You foulin' me up?" He yanked her toward him. Beneath his fingers, her shoulders remained rigid.

"I'm not going to marry you, Buzz. Not now. Not ever."

"You ain't going to marry me! Hey, what kind of a game is this?"

"It's no game. Go away. Buzz, before my father comes."

"Why you double-crossing little slut!" He started shaking her and he couldn't stop. His voice had risen almost to a scream. He was vaguely aware of the people in the lobby, that they were turning, staring.

He ought to watch his step, play it cool. But he couldn't control his burning fury. A red haze seemed to envelop him. It was like the other times he'd blown his top. Like when he'd socked the bandleader and got himself blacklisted. Like the time he'd walked out in the middle of a number because he'd got sore at a crack someone had made.

He heard his own voice rising shrilly, the words slurred and inarticulate. Then there was the impact of his hand slashing across Diane's face. The stinging sensation on his palm brought him back partially to his senses. He backed away a step and his hands dropped to his side.

An arm went around him roughly. He lunged, but fingers tightened on his wrist, drew his arm backward and upward, pinioning him fast. He turned enough to see that the man who held him was the doorman with the gold braid. He kicked back, but missed, and excruciating pain shot the length of his arm, making him gasp. The doorman loosened his grip and Buzz shot forward. His shoulder struck the padded leather. He slithered along the wall, almost falling. When he swung around, his teeth were bared, his face livid. The doorman stood in front of him, his features professionally blank, but with a glitter of battle in his eye.

Buzz's hand dipped into his pocket, came out with the blade. But before he snicked it open, a man stepped in between them and spoke in a crisp voice. "All right, Watkins, that's enough. I'll take care of this."

Buzz's eyes shifted to the newcomer. He was middle-aged, slight, almost delicate in appearance. The graying blond hair was combed carefully to one side and the features were fine-boned and regular. Buzz knew who he was, all right. He'd studied his pictures often enough in the tabloids. He'd expected a bigger man, more easy going in appearance. But it didn't take two guesses to tab him as Willis Griscom.

Buzz tried to pull himself together, even to give a shame-faced grin. But his face felt as though it had been starched. He knew his act wasn't going over, that nothing was going to do him any good. This cat was a real smooth customer, a guy who could see right through you with those chill blue eyes of his. Pulling anything on him would be like messing around with a charge of TNT.

All the same, he had to try. He wiped the back of his hand across his mouth. "Look, Mr. Griscom, this ain't the way it seems. Me and Diane are nuts about each other. We had a lover's quarrel and I lost my head." He could hear the whine in his own voice, but he couldn't stop. "Let's go somewhere and talk things over."

Griscom's lips quirked and his eyes flickered with contempt. He asked quietly, "What's your name, young man?"

Suddenly Buzz didn't want to tell him. He'd been having a pipe dream thinking he could put the black on Willis Griscom. He remembered the approach he'd worked out, half-threatening, half-conciliatory. And here he was with his back to the wall, panting for breath, and Griscom looking him over like he was dirt. This guy was too smooth; he'd outwit Buzz, toss him to the cops.

Buzz's eyes darted about him. The doorman had stepped back a little, but he was still ready for action. Diane was looking down at her feet, her face in profile strangely like her father's. There was a woman directly behind Griscom, tall, dark, svelte. Amusement showed in her brown eyes, and in the curve of her full lips. She put her hand on Griscom's arm, but he remained rigid.

Griscom spoke again, his voice icy. "All I've got to say to you, young man is this. Stay away from Diane."

Buzz felt the waves of fury beating over him again, drowning out his caution, his common sense. "Okay, maybe you'd like me to go to the cops. Maybe you'd like your name dragged in the mud. Maybe you'd—"

He stopped because Griscom wasn't even looking at him any longer. He had turned toward the doorman. "Watkins, I think we'd better have an officer here."

Watkins pivoted on his heel. Griscom wasn't bluffing, Buzz knew. A guy like Griscom would have the cops in his pocket. And once the fuzz latched on to him, Buzz didn't have a chance. There was only one thing to do—get out, but fast. He pushed forward blindly, half expecting Griscom to stop him. But there were no detaining hands, no footfalls behind him. Nothing. All the same, when he got into the clear, he began to run. He couldn't get out the door fast enough.

## 18

Buzz was still running when he hit Fifth Avenue. He lurched into a man and heard him swear. Buzz kept on moving fast but the incident sobered him a little. He quit running and started walking with long, loping strides.

The rage was still in him, ready to burst forth again if somebody crossed his path. His body was moist with sweat, his clothes sticking to him. He was mumbling to himself, and the muscles in his face were twitching. Anger caught in his throat and served to mask the lashing fear that was the real cause of his flight.

Everything had gone wrong just when he'd thought he'd set himself up solid. He had been just kidding himself; he couldn't stand up to a guy like Griscom, not without Diane's help. His anger veered to Diane. She was to blame for the whole rotten mess. Yeah, he had a score to settle with the two-timing little trim. His fists clenched so tightly that the muscles in his wrists throbbed. Once he got hold of that fancy two-bit piece, he'd really work her over.

No matter how you'd looked at it, Diane was to blame for all his troubles. If she hadn't tricked herself out to catch Nucci's eye, Nucci never would have come to his room, never killed Dottie. And Belle Foley's death—that could be laid at Diane's door too. Hadn't he made up to the Foley dame so he could swipe her car to protect Diane? Yeah, that's the way it was. Then after Diane had used him, got him all twisted up in her affairs, she'd tossed him out as though he were a plugged nickel. Worse than that, she'd made a monkey out of him in the lobby of the Piermont. But he'd fix her before he got through. He'd make her sorry she'd ever tried to play Buzz Baxter for a sucker.

In spite of himself, it was hard not to run. He was bumping into people again and that wasn't good. He had to cool off, think things over, plan what to do next. He forced himself to focus his attention on the sidewalk, to slow down, to look where he was going. He stopped on a corner, wondering how many blocks he'd walked, trying to orient himself. An old man was selling newspapers at a stand. Buzz's eyes picked out the screaming headlines six feet away: GIRL'S NUDE BODY FOUND ON MAITLAND ESTATE.

Dottie's picture nearly covered the front page. She was still wrapped in the blankets, so that only her face and the upper part of her body showed. He grabbed up the paper, holding it so tightly that it ripped beneath his fingers.

Someone plucked at his sleeve. The news vendor glared up at him. "Hey, mister, what's the matter with you? You wanna buy the paper or you wanna read it for free?"

Buzz fought the impulse to strike out at the old man's face. He flung down a coin and moved away. He'd have to get out of here, get some place alone to read the story. He started across the street toward the park. A taxi screamed to a halt, almost striking him. The driver shouted but Buzz scarcely noticed. He found an empty bench, spread the paper in front of him.

A grisly tragedy was revealed in the early hours of the morning when State Police found the body of a young girl secreted behind the house of Senator Maitland at Lymington-on-Hudson. The girl, estimated by police to be about sixteen years of age, died of multiple knife wounds. Her nude body, crudely wrapped in army blankets, had been dragged to a lane at the rear of the Maitland residence.

The crime was brought to light under bizarre circumstances. Several hours previously, Herbert Bailey, 68, caretaker on the estate, was awakened by the sounds of a car on the grounds. Mr. Bailey dressed hurriedly and went to investigate. As he approached the car, it shot forward, knocking him down and severely injuring him. Mr. Bailey was able to crawl to the street, where he was picked up by a passing motorist and taken to Lymington Hospital, where it was found he was suffering from two broken ribs, a broken arm and numerous contusions.

The State Police were called and checked the scene of the crime. There they found what at first seemed to be an old roll of blankets. When this was opened, a girl's body was revealed. She had apparently died from knife wounds. Six deep slashes were found on the lower portions of her body and her left breast. There was also discoloration about her throat.

At present the girl has not been identified, but it is believed that she was killed elsewhere and brought to Lymington in the car which struck down the caretaker. Mr. Bailey was unable to give any description of the car or its occupants.

Neither Senator Maitland, who was reached by telephone in Paris, or any member of his family was able to shed the slightest light on the mystery.

Buzz read the story three times. It could be worse. As long as they didn't know who Dottie was, they couldn't tie either Nucci or himself to the crime. But what about Diane? When she saw the picture, maybe her nerves would crack. Maybe she'd put in a squeal to the cops to save her own neck. Even worse, she might spill the story to her father. She might have done that already. He'd have to reach her, make sure she kept her trap shut. But that wasn't going to be easy. She wasn't dreamy-eyed over him any longer. There was only one way to make sure she didn't run off at the mouth, and that was to silence her forever.

A strange excitement took hold of him. Suddenly he understood about Nucci, why he'd kept driving the knife into Dottie. And that gave him another idea. Last night he'd almost cooked Nucci's goose. If Dottie had stayed away from his pad, Nucci would be dead now and Buzz in the clear. Okay, he'd worked it out once. Why not set it up all over again?

It would take some planning, but he was good at that. Last night he'd got some lousy breaks and everybody had double crossed him. He'd learned one thing. Never trust anybody. It was Buzz Baxter alone against the rest of the world.

The thought did something to him, puffed him up, gave him courage. All he needed was a reefer to make things really fleecy. He searched through the pockets of his tweed jacket before he remembered his decision not to bring any boom along to his talk with Willis Griscom. He patted his wallet. It was lucky he still had plenty of the folding stuff he'd lifted from Gladys Maintree. He could go down to Times Square and buy himself a supply, or go up to Spanish Harlem to see Riffy. But it would be easier to go to his room, where he had about six sticks stuck away.

A tremor of anxiety passed through him. He shouldn't have left the pad for so long. Not with the cops swarming over the house. He'd better head uptown right away. He had plenty to do as soon as he got back. He'd have to clean up the place so that if the nosy rookie decided to sniff around there wouldn't be anything for him to find. The nerves in his fingertips started humming. He'd been so sore about the way things had gone with Griscom that he'd scarcely given a thought to Belle Foley. But if the cops had found his fingerprints on the glass, they'd be on his tail. Right now they might be sitting in his room waiting for him.

Maybe he shouldn't go back at all. Maybe he should dig a hole for himself and climb in. But that was nuts. Once he took it on the lam, the spotlight would be on him. He'd have to find out how the land lay, and the sooner he got back to his pad the better.

He grabbed a cab but he told the driver to drop him off a block and a half from his house. He walked along cautiously, keeping an eye out for trouble. He was wasting his time. The block was quiet except for some kids playing stickball in the street. You'd never know by the look of things that there'd been any excitement here in the morning. Hell, the cops had probably crossed Belle Foley out hours ago. They couldn't investigate every drunken dame who cashed in her tickets when she had a snootful.

The building was silent as a tomb without the sound of Foley's radio to liven it up. Buzz moved softly down the hall, listened at his door. He unlocked it and went inside. The place was just the way he'd left it. He let out his breath. It showed how you could get the wind up over nothing.

He got a reefer burning and started cleaning up the room. He went to work on the bloodstain first, swabbing at it with the stained towel he'd used earlier. Then he laid Dottie's clothes on the table. All cheap stuff—the kind you could buy anywhere. He snipped off a label and a couple of laundry marks and stuffed the clothing into an old pillow slip. He could stash the bundle away in a locker until he got a chance to toss it in the river. He stuck a heavy book end among the clothes to add weight. His attention switched to the mattress. He turned it over and looked at the stains. They were worse than he'd realized. But what could you do about a mattress? You couldn't walk out of here with a bloody mattress on your back.

He got another idea. He went to the window and looked out. Belle Foley's Ford was still in the mews, and it didn't look as though it had been touched. He let himself out the rear door and approached the car. It was mud-spattered from last night's trip. The key was still in the ignition lock. Probably the cops hadn't even bothered to check to see if Foley owned a car.

She wasn't the sort of dame you'd expect to have one. Still, they must have found her driver's license in her purse.

He had to get the mattress out of his room, and here was a chance. But shouldn't he wait until dark? He wavered uncertainly. No one was in the mews, no one at the windows. He climbed into the car and turned on the ignition. The motor purred softly. He eased the Ford around so that it was only a few feet from the back door. He left the motor running and returned to his room. He doubled up the thin mattress under his arm and picked up the pillow case. He took them to the Ford and dumped them down in back. He was just slipping in behind the wheel when he heard footsteps on the cobbled alleyway that led to the mews.

He couldn't decide whether to make a run for it or brazen it out. And then it was too late. The rookie cop was there at the bend, looking directly at him. The cop's mouth opened to give a yell, but Buzz didn't hear it. He gunned the motor and the roar drowned out every other sound.

It was as if last night were repeating itself. The Ford shot forward, rushing toward the figure in its path. But the cop's reactions were faster than the old man's had been. He flung himself to one side, plastered himself against the brick wall of the building. Buzz's face was only an inch or two from the back of the cop's head as he slithered by.

He clamped his hands to the wheel and twisted with all his might. The back fender hit the corner of the building with a grinding slap that jarred the whole car. He pressed hard on the gas and felt the car rip free. He jolted into the alleyway, double-kicked into high and hit the road wide open.

He was racing the wrong way along a one-way street, but he didn't have far to go. A truck rounded the corner. Brakes screamed as Buzz fought the wheel, trying to slide by. Metal crashed and the Ford swerved dangerously to the left, its front wheels mounting the sidewalk. Buzz swung back into the roadway and shot north up the avenue.

He nosed into the line of heavy traffic, breathing hard, not daring to look behind. He was safe for a while. It took a long time to throw out a net for a car. The engine began to cough. Buzz looked down at the gas register. The arrow pointed to empty. The Ford was slowing down already. Other cars were circling around him. Buzz glanced ahead. No gas stations. He gave a little whimpering cry as the motor died. He twisted around, searching the avenue for signs of pursuit. What he saw sent a chill along his spine. The rear window of the Ford was starred with a bullet hole. The rookie cop must have snapped a shot.

He was out of the car now and on the road, running as soon as his feet touched the asphalt. He didn't know where he was going, didn't care as long as he put distance between himself and the car. A subway kiosk loomed up ahead of him. He darted down the stairs. He didn't have a token, and it seemed that he stood for an eternity in front of the cashier's cage, waiting for him to make change, to push the tokens across the counter.

A train was just drawing into the platform. Buzz's hand shook so that he could hardly fit the token into the slot. Finally he stumbled across the platform and caught the door of the train as it was closing. He forced his fingers into the crack, pushed the door back and squeezed inside. He leaned against the door, wanting to sob.

At the next station some of the seats emptied. He slumped down into a corner. The car filled up again, then pitched forward in its rocky passage. Buzz pressed against the framework beside him, feeling some strange comfort in its metallic hardness. After a while the clatter and bang of the car, the voices around him, and the swaying movement seemed to cover him, conceal him, wrap him up as though in a cocoon. He was all right here; nobody ever paid any attention to you on a subway. All he had to do now was stay here forever. He raised his face for a moment and looked around dazedly. Then he leaned back and closed his eyes.

## 19

Diane let the bus carry her past her hotel, under Washington Arch and into the Square. She got off slowly and wandered aimlessly about the park, not wanting to return to the hotel to face her mother.

In her mind she went over the scene in the lobby of the Piermont—Buzz's hands rough on her shoulders, his breath hot on her face, the swift, unwanted flame of desire that might have made her give way to him if her father had not interrupted at the crucial moment. She had heard the truculence and anger in Buzz's voice, but she had recognized the fear that lay beneath it....

She didn't dare to look at him when he was shouting at her father. Buzz, with his mercurial shifts of mood, his insecurity betraying itself in bursts of temper, in extremes of elation or depression, was no match for the frigid control, the icy temperament of her father. She had wanted to tell that to Buzz last night, but she had known there was no way to make him understand. At the last moment, there in the hotel lobby, if Buzz had pleaded with her to go with him, she might have done so. Not so much because of the way she felt about Buzz but as an act of defiance against her father, as a symbol of hatred for the woman who had stood beside him.

She watched Buzz run to the doorway and as always when she saw him in flight, she had the impulse to run with him, to call his name. She even took a step toward him, but her father seized her wrist. She tried to draw away, but his fingers were like steel.

"What's going on, Diane? How'd you pick up with a cheap little hoodlum like that? Haven't you any sense at all?"

She stopped struggling and averted her face. Then she heard her stepmother's voice, the tones too dulcet. "Don't be too severe with her, Willis. After all, she's only a child."

"All right, all right. Let's find a place where we can talk things over. I want to hear all about this young man." Diane looked at him and then her eyes flickered to the woman. She saw the curve of the full lips, the little mocking smile. Her stepmother said, "You know, he's rather handsome in a flashy sort of way, but—"

Griscom's words cut her off. "That's enough, Claire. First of all, I want this young man's name."

Diane drew herself straight. "I won't tell you. I won't tell you anything at all. You had your chance, and you wouldn't listen. Now it's too late. You say he's cheap. All right so he's cheap, but what kind of a woman did you pick?"

The blood drained from her father's face. For a moment, she thought he would strike her. But when she stepped toward him, he moved back and let her by. She walked on, through the door through which Buzz had passed and out into the street. She half hoped that Buzz would be outside waiting for her, but when she looked there was no sign of him.

She stood uncertainly in the bright sunlight. Maybe she should go to Buzz's room, but she sensed he wouldn't return there. Not right away. She'd have to find him soon. Whatever the pattern of their relationship, it wasn't ended. It was like a musical number that broke off with a jagged beat. The tune would have to be picked up again, brought to a climactic ending.

Listlessness crept over her, numbing her body. She closed her mind to the future and, walking automatically, crossed the street to the bus stop and boarded the next bus that came along....

Now here she was in Washington Square, the broad avenue stretching before her. There was nothing to do but go home. She walked slowly, her eyes on the glaring pavement.

The shadow moving beside hers caught her eye first; then she heard the voice. "Diane."

She stopped, poised for flight. At first the face seemed that of a stranger. Then she recognized Johnnie Lacy.

"I've been waiting for you, Diane."

"You've been waiting? Why?"

"I thought maybe you were in trouble. I thought maybe I could help."

She tried to keep her voice level, but she couldn't prevent the tremor in it. "Trouble? What made you think that?"

"Have you seen the afternoon papers?" He spread the tabloid out in front of her. A girl's face, the eyes closed in death, covered the front page.

She gasped. "It's Dottie. Dottie Marr." She clung to him for a moment, fighting back the nausea that threatened to engulf her. She'd have to pull herself together. She said quickly, "What's it all got to do with me, Johnnie?"

Johnnie's tones were apologetic. "Nothing, I hope. But you've got to know sooner or later, Dottie was Buzz's girlfriend. When they identify her, Buzz is going to be on the dime."

"Buzz didn't kill her."

"Nobody's said he did. Not yet, at least. But Dottie was around the Green Elephant last night, higher than a kite, telling everybody she was going to queer Buzz' pitch with you. Once the cops hear that they're going to be buzzing around you thicker than bees."

Diane bit her lip. "Maybe the police will never find out who she is."

Johnnie shook his head. "The crowd Dottie hung around with are cop-shy. Most of them are on the needle and they wouldn't walk within a block of a station. But sooner or later someone's going to tip off the police. Besides—"

"What are you trying to tell me, Johnnie?"

"Dottie was a junkie, maybe worse. But she didn't deserve this. I guess I've got a duty to go to the cops."

"No, Johnnie. Please."

Johnnie's gaze dropped. "You were with Buzz last night. I wasn't snooping. I just happened to pass the Pleasure Palace when you met him. That's why I came to you before calling the cops."

"You've got to believe me. Buzz didn't kill Dottie.

Nucci did."

"Nucci! How do you know?"

"I was with Buzz when he discovered the body." She hesitated, studying Johnnie's face, then reached a quick decision. "I'll tell you about it if you promise to help."

"Suppressing evidence is dangerous stuff. It's playing with dynamite."

Diane's lip twisted in scorn. "Aren't you noble, Johnnie! Why don't you call the cops to come and arrest me now?"

"Hey, cut it out. I didn't say no. I was just thinking out loud. If you're mixed up in this, Diane, I'll go out on a limb for you. But not for Buzz."

"All I ask is that you keep quiet. Give Buzz as much time as you can."

"I can't do it, baby. Not unless I know what the score is."

"All right, I guess I'll have to tell you." She started walking back toward the Square. Johnnie's footsteps rang on the pavement beside her but she kept her eyes straight ahead, not wanting to look at him. In Washington Square she found an empty bench out of earshot of the old men who lounged nearby. She dropped down on it and Johnnie took a seat beside her.

She'd have to tell it straight, she decided, from beginning to end. Johnnie knew about Nucci anyway, about her meeting with Buzz last night. She glanced up at him quickly. "Why do you want to help me, Johnnie?"

His grin was crooked. He spread his hands. "I'm just a moonstruck goon, Diane. There's something about you that sends me. But don't get me wrong. I'm not trying to cut in on Buzz. Not that I wouldn't like to. But I know I don't stand a chance."

"You're sweet, Johnnie."

He rested his hand on hers and she let it remain there. She began to talk, watching his face, wondering how much she could trust him when the chips were down. She didn't have much choice, she thought bitterly. If Buzz were caught now, he'd pull her down with him. And if the police arrested Nucci, he'd destroy them all. Johnnie would have to know the truth or he would light the fuse that would start the chain reaction.

As she talked she studied his expression. First anger, then incredulity and finally indecision showed in his face. When she had finished, he said, "We can't hold this back. Nucci's a psycho. If he killed Dottie, he's likely to kill again. Then we'd be responsible."

"It's a chance we've got to take."

"Did you think who his next victim might be? He's got a yen for you, Diane. And he's a killer. That's the way he gets his kicks."

"There's no proof that Nucci murdered Dottie—only my word and Buzz's. How far will that go with the police?"

"If Buzz is in the clear, why should you worry? They'll be able to set the time of death. Probably it was while you were both at the Moontime. Sure, Buzz has a record, but what makes him think the cops will frame him? They'd be as anxious to collar Nucci as anyone."

"You're forgetting that we moved the body. We ran down the old man in the Maitland estate. Both of us were there. Buzz and myself."

"It's bad, but the cops are going to tumble to it in the end. The sooner Buzz speaks up the better. Besides, until this thing is cleared up, Buzz is going to be frantic and I know Buzz—when he's in a frenzy he's capable of anything. It's better to have him in custody for a crime he didn't commit than for him to be on the loose. When he blows his top, he's likely to dig a grave for himself."

"What about me, Johnnie?"

"You're not in so deep you can't pull out. Go back to your father. Tell him what you've just told me. Griscom has plenty of drag."

"No. I won't do it."

"Okay, I can't make you. But Buzz can be a real bad joe. One promise I've got to have, that you won't see him alone again. If he wants to meet you, let me tag along."

"What good will that do?"

"I can handle Buzz. Listen to me, Diane. I don't want to crowd you, but the idea of your wandering around on your own gives me the shudders. I promised I wouldn't go to the cops, but if I'm not in the picture, I'm going to see Griscom."

Diane studied the stubborn face. She nodded. "All right, Johnnie, I promise."

She let him take her back to the hotel. She let herself into the apartment quietly. Her mother was sitting by the window. She looked up and started to rise. Diane ran into her own room and bolted the door. She could hear Iris calling to her, hear the soft pounding of her hands on the panel, but she didn't answer. She lay down on the bed, burying her face in her crossed arms.

# 20

Buzz couldn't stay in the subway forever, no matter how much he wanted to. He looked at his watch. He'd been riding back and forth for hours. It would be dark outside now, and darkness gave some safety. The train jolted to a stop at Grand Central. This was no place to get off. If the word were out to pick him up, the first spot the cops would stake off would be the station. He forced himself to settle back against the seat. He rode two stops, getting off at 59th.

It was dark, all right, and chilly, with a Scotch mist that set his teeth chattering. He hurried into a greasy spoon, bought himself coffee and sat at the counter, sipping the hot, bitter brew and trying to think out his next move. He couldn't go back to his pad, and the Times Square area would be risky. He'd better stay off Swing Street, too. The rookie cop knew he was a musician.

Pretty soon he'd have to load up on boom, but right now he needed sleep more than anything else. He wondered if the cops had put out an alarm for him. He saw the tabloid in a booth and went over and got it. The finding of Dottie's body was still in the headlines but there was nothing new. She hadn't been identified. On an inside page was an article he almost missed. Belle Foley's death was announced. According to the story she "had fallen or been pushed." The last paragraph contained a guarded statement from the district attorney's office, saying that "certain peculiar circumstances regarding Mrs. Foley's death were being investigated."

Buzz's shaking fingers made the paper rattle and he laid it down on the counter. There was nothing in the tabloid to indicate that the police had linked Belle Foley's death with Dottie's murder. But that meant only that the cops were playing their cards close to the chest. It couldn't have taken them long to guess that the bloody mattress and the girl's clothing that he'd left in the abandoned Ford had some significance. And with the story about Dottie on the front page, they'd be morons if they didn't start adding things up.

Hanging around the brightly lit café was crazy. What he had to do was find a place to cat up. But where? Registering at a hotel would be like sticking his head into a noose. Tomorrow maybe he could find a room somewhere, a place where they wouldn't ask questions. He still had plenty of folding stuff. Over a hundred dollars was left from the bread he'd lifted from Gladys Maintree.

Maintree—that gave him a thought. He'd spent one night with her. Why not another? No one would ever think of looking for him in a ritzy dive like Maintree's apartment. He'd be safe there. He couldn't help grinning; he'd worked out a perfect setup without even half trying.

Maintree's place wasn't far. It would be better to walk it than to take a cab. Half the drivers in town were police buffs, ready to sell you down the river for an in with the cops. He started off, walking jauntily. The mist was dank but it made a good cover. No one could spot you more than a foot away.

He turned in under the marquee and strode through the foyer. The desk clerk was the cat he knew, the one he'd slipped some fins to. The elevator boy was new, probably taking Luis's place. He started to step into the elevator but the operator blocked his way. "Sorry, sir, but are you a resident?"

"I'm going to Miss Maintree's apartment."

"You have to clear with the desk, sir."

Buzz swung around. He'd like to knock the guy's face off but it wouldn't do to blow his top. Besides, the desk clerk would clear him in a second.

Buzz said, "Hi. Tell the punk over there to take me to sixteen."

The desk clerk looked at him without any sign of recognition. His round, pale face was blank. "I'll have to have your name, sir, to announce you."

"Don't hand me that crap. You know Maintree wants to see me."

"The management has given strict orders, sir."

Buzz took out his wallet, put a five on the counter. The desk clerk didn't touch it. His glance slid to the corner of the lobby. Buzz turned. A big guy was sitting there. A house dick, Buzz guessed. He said, "Okay, just tell her Buzz is here."

He watched while the room clerk rang. The clerk spoke too softly for Buzz to distinguish the words but he heard the crackle of Maintree's voice.

The clerk hung up, came over to him. "I'm sorry. Miss Maintree says she's not to be disturbed."

It took a minute for the message to register. Maintree didn't want to see him. That meant that she had a new contact, that Spasm had somebody else covering Buzz's route. Otherwise Maintree would be screaming for him to come up. A wave of fury hit him. He grabbed at the desk clerk's coat, "Goddamn you, let me go up."

The clerk tried to back away but Buzz clung to him, dragging him so close that their faces were less than an inch apart. The man's pale eyes bulged with terror. Buzz yelled, "What you think you're pulling, jerk? You've taken plenty of fins off me. Now I want up. So pass the word along."

A heavy hand spun him about. It was the big house dick who'd been in the corner. In his anger, Buzz had forgotten all about him. The dick spoke out of the corner of his mouth. "Outside, buster. Get moving."

Buzz was shaking with rage, but he knew he'd have to go. If there were a hassle here the cops would be on his neck in no time flat. He managed a shrug. "Okay—okay."

He was still burning when he hit the avenue. He started walking aimlessly. Then he realized he was headed back for the bright lights. He stopped to consider. What he needed right now was some boom, but Times Square wasn't the place to score. There was a dive near Columbus Circle where he could buy the stuff. The cat overcharged you and panned off beat stuff whenever he thought he could get away with it. But Buzz knew the angles. He'd get what he wanted.

He crossed Fifth Avenue and entered Central Park. The anger churning within him made his temples throb and his legs weak. But he didn't dare stop moving. After a while his breath started to choke him and he had to slow down. Only then was he aware of the footsteps behind him, matching his own.

Who was there in the darkness? A cop? Nucci? He ought to run, but he knew he wouldn't get far. His legs were like rubber and he was already gasping. There was a light a dozen yards ahead. If he could make it, he'd swing around there and face his pursuer.

He forced himself to sprint for the light. He hadn't been mistaken. Whoever was behind him was running too. He reached the arc of light and turned, his fists clenched. The figure behind him stopped where the shadow of a tree fell across his face.

It wasn't Nucci, or a cop, either. But who the hell was the guy? Whoever he was, he was short. He wouldn't come up to Buzz's shoulder. The figure moved forward cautiously. He looked like a boy, not fully grown. Was he a mugger? Buzz caught a glint of light on a knife blade. Instinctively he reached for his own switchblade. The boy moved in a few steps. There was something familiar about him, but Buzz couldn't think where he'd seen him before. Then he almost laughed aloud. Luis Mercado—he hadn't recognized him without his monkey suit. Hell, what was the punk trying to pull? Buzz could handle him with one hand tied behind his back.

He said, "Hello, Luis. I thought you was in the slammer."

Luis stopped, then edged a bit closer. "Not me. I made bail. I ain't got no record. Since I got out, I been looking for you."

"What for? To get your spine ripped out?"

"You lifted the stuff from Maintree, not me."

"They found you loaded, didn't they?"

"A couple of costume pieces. You got the heavy ice."

"What do you want me to do? Go crying to the cops that you was a good boy, that you took only my leavings?"

"To hell with that. You mailed me the watch to try to frame me. You would have too, except my brother got hold of it. But I'm shanking you for the try, you dirty bastard."

"Nobody's holding you. Come on, if you're so brave."

Buzz caught the movement of shadow to his right.

He knew now why Luis had been stalling. Someone was circling him, coming up in back. Buzz turned just in time to see the figure hurtling toward him, a boy who looked like Luis, probably his brother. Buzz's arm swung low, ready to rip upward with the switchblade. But a third figure launched itself at his back. Buzz fell forward, his knife clattering on the concrete. He felt metal slice into his forearm. He tried to get up, but a heavy blow across his neck sent him sprawling again. Sharp-toed shoes drummed against his ribs, crashed into the side of his head. He seemed to be whirling into a bottomless pit. Then something soft and cool seemed to drop over him, easing his pain, leaving nothing but blackness.

He couldn't have blacked out long because he could hear the sound of running feet when he returned to consciousness. He rolled to one side and the slashing pain brought an involuntary cry to his lips. From somewhere not far away there issued the shrill blast of a police whistle. He'd have to get out of here, but fast, or the cops would pick him up. The pain was sending tongues of fire through his body, but there wasn't time to think about that now. Somehow he had to get away.

He dragged himself to a bench, pulled himself up. The pain made him dizzy and he nearly collapsed again, but he couldn't be taken now. He began to stagger across the grass, clutching at his ribs, bent over almost double. After a few steps, he managed a jarring dogtrot.

It seemed miles to Columbus Circle. He fell down half a dozen times. Once he lay still for a long time, unable to get up. He'd fallen in the shadow of a clump of bushes. He pushed himself up with his hands, the effort starting a spasm of retching. When the sickness had passed he felt able to navigate again.

He could see the neon sign of Jimmy's Place ahead of him. Once he got there, he'd buy himself enough boom so that he'd be soaring. Yeah, he'd climb right over the Empire State Building. He'd stay high for a week.

Only half a block to go. The thought of the boom kept him on his feet. The door of Jimmy's was open. He staggered through, propped himself against the bar. His hand went to his breast pocket. Spread out the folding stuff, he told himself, get the boom quick. Then he stared incredulously at his empty hand. He searched frantically through his other pockets. Forty cents in change, a subway token. That was all. Luis had got the rest.

He swore out loud. Then he caught his image reflected in the long-cracked mirror behind the bar. He scarcely recognized himself. His face was smeared with dirt and one eye was puffed. The sleeve of his tweed jacket had been ripped nearly to the elbow and was caked with blood. He couldn't stay here. As soon as the bartender came along, he'd start asking questions, maybe call the nabs. He'd have to move again, find himself a place where it was dark and nobody would see him. But this time he wouldn't run. He was too tired for that.

## 21

Diane awakened with a start. The room was dark except for the irregular rectangles of yellowish light that poured through her windows and spread unevenly across her bed. She raised her head, listening. There was only the roar of traffic and muted voices rising from the street. But she was sure that a noise close at hand had aroused her.

A shrill tinkling echoed feebly through the room. Automatically she reached for the telephone, then her hand drew back. It wasn't the phone, but the doorbell. She got up hastily and unbolted the door of her room. The foyer beyond was dark. As she stopped uncertainly, a light snapped on in her mother's room.

Diane hurried to the door leading to the corridor and leaned against it. There was another noise, a brittle scrabbling sound like fingernails clawing at the wooden panel. She called out, "Who is it?"

"Diane, let me in."

She didn't recognize the hoarse whisper. Could it be Nucci with another of his tricks? She called again, "Who's there?"

"Me . . . Buzz. I'm hurt."

She hesitated for only a moment, then flung the door open. He was leaning against the wall, half-crouching. First she saw his eyes, sunken, gleaming, and his mouth twisted with pain. Then her gaze dropped to his blood-encrusted sleeve. He stumbled past her, heeled the door shut, and stood swaying in front of her. "I had to come to you, Diane. There wasn't nobody else."

"What happened?"

"I got mugged. Shanked and rolled."

He flopped onto a divan in the foyer and stared up at her, his eyes red-rimmed. She said, "I'll phone a doctor."

"To hell with that. I'm on the run, baby, and a sawbones might turn me in."

She tried to examine his arm but he jerked away. "That can wait. What I need now is bread."

"Bread?"

"Yeah, folding stuff. Money to you."

"But, Buzz, your arm—"

"Quit kicking it around. You going to help me or ain'tcha? I tell you it's dough I need."

"I haven't much. Only a few dollars."

"Even that'll help. It'll buy me a scratch for the night. I gotta get under cover."

Diane straightened up and saw that her mother had come to the outer edge of the foyer. The light behind her made her plump figure appear enormous. The pudgy face, without make-up, was dead white, the eyes big with fear. "What's wrong, Diane? Who's this man?"

Diane's eyes flicked to Buzz. She caught the warning in his expression. She spoke crisply. "There's nothing to worry about. Buzz is a friend of mine. He was held up just outside. He's been hurt a little."

"The police. We ought to—"

Buzz broke in hoarsely. "No. For God's sake, no cops."

Diane touched his shoulder and said to Iris. "If the police come, they'll question us all night. Besides, the hotel wouldn't like it."

She saw Iris's hands flutter in a helpless gesture, and she knew she'd won her point. Iris hated bother of any kind. She swung about and started for her own room. Buzz followed her.

She crossed to the bureau on which her purse lay. Before she reached it Buzz grabbed her by the shoulders, spun her around. "What about your old woman? Maybe she's yacking to the nabs right now."

"No. She's too frightened. But I'd better go to her."

"Do that. Make sure she keeps her trap shut."

Diane went back to the foyer. Her mother was still standing where she had left her. Diane took her arm, propelled her back to her own room. Iris was shaking uncontrollably. Diane said sharply, "Pull yourself together, Mother. Buzz was robbed and he put up a fight. That's all there is to it."

"Why did he come here? He frightens me."

"They took all his money. I'll give him enough for a taxi home. He'll be gone in a few minutes."

Iris began to wring her hands. "I don't know, the way you've been acting. Now, this man."

"Stop it, Mother. As soon as he goes, I'll come back and tell you everything." She kissed Iris lightly on the temple and saw her face brighten. Her mother's plump hand came up to embrace her but Diane moved away quickly.

As she entered her room, she saw that Buzz had dumped the contents of her purse on the bureau top. The little roll of bills was gone, even the change. He had taken a seat on the edge of her bed and was fumbling with the knobs of the radio. Music flooded the room for an instant, then was cut off by an announcer's voice. Buzz turned the radio down to a whisper. He leaned forward, so intent on what he was doing that she was sure he had not heard her.

She missed the first part of the announcement. But as she drew near she could hear plainly: "Police tonight are searching for Byron 'Buzz' Baxter to question him concerning the mysterious death of Mrs. Belle Foley. Baxter first aroused the suspicions of Patrolman Timothy O'Toole when he—"

Buzz looked up and saw her. His face darkened and he snapped off the radio.

She asked breathlessly, "Who's Belle Foley?"

He stared at her without speaking, his face swollen and lopsided, his eyes slits. Finally he said, "Just an old witch that lived up at my place. She was riding a broom last night and fell off."

"Stop it, Buzz. I've got to know the truth."

"No, you ain't, sugar. Foley ain't none of your affair. The less you know about her, the fewer chances of spilling."

She bit her lip but remained silent. He unclenched his fist, showing the wad of bills. He said, "Only fourteen bucks. It ain't going to carry me far."

"It's all I've got.

"Can't you knock the old woman up for ten?"

"Not tonight. She's too upset."

He shrugged and stood up. He reached out to embrace her but she shrank away. His eyes glittered with anger but when he spoke his voice was almost wheedling. "I gotta beat it, baby, before I suck the cops in here. I don't know where I'm headin' but I'll hole up somewhere." He waited for her to answer. When she remained silent, he said, "I'm really in a hot spot. You ain't going to turn on me, sugar? You'll help me out, won't you?"

"I guess so."

"That's my baby. All I need's some folding stuff. With enough dough, I can keep under wraps until this thing blows over. Can you get it for me? I'll pay you back as soon as I can."

"How much do you need?"

"As much as you can lay your hands on."

"I don't know how much that will be. Will a hundred dollars do?"

"I guess it'll have to. But I don't dare come here

again. I tell you what, I'll phone you, meet you somewhere. Don't let me down, baby."

"I'll have the money for you."

"Solid. You'll be hearing from me." He leaned forward and kissed her quickly. She didn't draw back this time, but remained motionless, watching him as he went out through the door. He moved soundlessly, almost like a cat. She waited, expecting to hear the outer door close, but the minutes clicked by and there was only silence.

She crossed the room and looked out into the dark foyer. Buzz was silhouetted against the light of her mother's doorway. He froze at sight of her. Then he took two hurried steps to the outer door, wrenched it open and slipped out into the corridor. The door closed after him with a little slam.

When he had gone, Diane hurried to her mother's room. It was empty and Diane heard the sound of running water in the bathroom. She looked around quickly. The upper drawer of her mother's dresser was partly open. The piles of nightdresses and underclothing were slightly rumpled. What had Buzz been searching for? Money? Jewelry? What did it matter? She smoothed out the ruffled clothing and shut the drawer just as her mother entered the room.

## 22

Fourteen bucks in his pocket and no place to go. Still things could be a lot worse. With fourteen bucks he could pad down for the night and buy himself a couple of packs of reefers. There was something else in his pocket that made him feel good. When he'd left

Diane, he'd seen her mother's room was lighted up and the old woman wasn't there. He'd just stepped in to take a look-see. Maybe she'd left her purse around or some jewelry that he could hock. But he didn't see anything of value.

He'd pulled open the drawer of her dresser just for luck, and had run his hands through the slips and underclothes. And there it was down at the bottom of the drawer. A neat little pearl-handled revolver. He picked it up, hefted it. It was light but perfectly balanced, a tiny French model that fitted snugly in his hand. He cracked it open to make sure that it was loaded and slipped it into his pocket.

Diane had caught him in the snooping act. But he couldn't care less. She had to play ball with him whether she wanted to or not. Besides the gun really made him feel good. It took away some of the feeling of helplessness he'd had ever since Luis and his goons had stripped him of his dough. After all, a guy with a joint was something to be reckoned with.

After he'd walked a block or two the bravado went out of him. He thought he caught people staring at his bloody sleeve and his puffed face. He sidled into the shadows and at the next corner he turned into a side street.

He'd been walking too fast, and the pain started knifing into him again, striking along his arm and across his ribs where Luis had kicked him. His head felt light and his legs went all rubbery. He'd better find a subway quick. There ought to be a kiosk somewhere near but he couldn't see any. He stumbled, caught himself against a rusted railing and let himself down on a step.

He didn't dare stay very long or some cop would

come along and start asking questions. He'd have to use his noodle if he was getting out of this caper without landing in stir. But hell, how could you think when your head was going around and around and your stomach was churning? He'd have to straighten himself and find a place to kip. But first he needed some boom.

The thought of the boom filled him with a rising excitement. Riffy's was the place to go. You didn't have to be afraid of anyone calling the nabs in Spanish Harlem. The cats up there didn't want any truck with the cops. He ought to take the subway but the thought of the grinding, jolting ride, the strange impersonal faces staring at him, gave him the shivers. A bus would be even worse. A taxi would set him back a couple bucks, but it would be worth it.

He hailed a cab at Broadway and gave the driver the address of the sleazy nightclub where Riffy hung out. Before they'd gone half a dozen blocks he was nodding, and he didn't wake up until the cabby yelled at him.

He found Riffy right away, which was good. If he'd had to comb the turf he would have conked off. He scored in the washroom and went out in the alley for his drags. The stuff was beat, dark-brown and harsh, but it smoothed him out, took some of the pain away.

He went back into the club. There wasn't an orchestra, but a Puerto Rican cat was messing around with a beat-up piano. Latin stuff, with a crazy lilt to it. The guy shadowed the tune, circled around it, then licked it out fast. He was a square, strictly from nowhere. Buzz lost interest and his eyes wandered around the room. A couple of cuties were at the bar. He could pick one of them up, get himself a flop. But it was risky. These kinds looked like jailbait. Even if their jelly boys didn't roll him, they'd probably toss him out before morning.

Then the idea hit him and he wondered why it had taken so long. Nucci. He'd planned to make a fresh deal with Nucci. Why not tonight? Nucci would have to help him cat up even if he didn't want to. Nucci couldn't afford to have the cops grab him. The zombie had his own skin to think of.

Nucci's place wasn't far, six or seven blocks. Buzz began to walk it. He was feeling fleecy now and the thudding pain was reduced to a mild aching that was almost pleasurable. He kept dragging at his reefer as he walked along. He knew it was a crazy thing to do but he didn't care. The reaction to his panic had set in. He was feeling big, reckless, powerful.

He found Nucci's place, climbed the high stoop and pushed open the door to the grimy hallway. He kept on moving, up the stairs, along the corridor to Nucci's door. His fist hammered on the door. Boards cracked inside the room, then there was silence. Nucci was there, all right. Buzz pictured him standing half dressed in the room, frozen in alarm, wondering whether to crawl through the window or to try to fight his way out. The picture brought a gurgle of laughter to his lips which in turn sent tongues of fire through his chest.

Nucci opened the door a crack, stared at him with one eye. "What ya doing here?"

"Lemme in. Let's dig it for a while."

Nucci thought it over, then he opened the door. The place wasn't the way Buzz had imagined it at all. It was neat as a pin, barren as a prison cell. No nudies on the wall. The bed made up like an army cot. A straight-back chair drawn up to an empty table.

"You picked yourself a real hip monastery, Nucci."

"Shut up, you double-crossing punk."

Buzz could see the shank in Nucci's hand, the hilt covered by his spatulate fingers, the blade extending eight inches beyond his palm. He said, "I didn't cross you, Nucci. I brought the girl like I promised. Why'd you have to beat the gong and shag Dottie?"

Nucci's tongue slid over his gray lips. "I thought she was the Griscom trim and then she started hollering. I had to keep her quiet, didn't I?"

No sense arguing with this psycho. You couldn't tell when he'd flip and let go at you with his shank. Buzz spoke softly. "You still want the fancy stuff?"

Nucci licked his lips again. "Yeah. That dame does things to me. She's class."

"I can still fix it up, Nucci. But you gotta help me. I need a pad for the night. The cops are on my tail. They catch up with me, it's going to be curtains for you."

Nucci gave a little laugh. "You learn fast, don't you, Buzz? You and me, we're like Siamese twins. One of us takes the hot squat, the other gets burned too."

Buzz tried to keep the tremor out of his voice. "Okay, twin, what about shaking me up a room?"

Nucci thought it over, then he jerked his head for Buzz to follow. He led him into the hall, up the stairs to a room immediately above his own. The rooms were replicas, a cot, a bureau, a table and a straight-back chair. The window looked out on a brick wall.

Nucci turned to look at Buzz. "You're safe here. You don't need to see nobody. I'll tell the guy who runs the joint a pal of mine is here. That's all."

"Thanks, twin."

"Cut out the comedy routine."

Buzz shrugged. The guy still had the shank in his hand, and Buzz didn't want to tangle with him. He waited, but Nucci remained standing underneath the naked bulb. After a while Buzz asked, "Something bothering you?"

"Yeah. About the dame. You wouldn't be kidding me, would ya?"

"I'm leveling."

Nucci grunted. "You better be, sonny, because I been thinkin' maybe I'd be better off if you wasn't around. Some punks know too much and squeal too easy. Punks like that wake up sometimes with a knife in their backs."

What the hell, was the creep going to stay here all night, making with the threats? Buzz's fingers twitched. His high was wearing off and the pain was flooding back into his body. But he didn't want to light up in front of Nucci.

He turned his back, pulled down the blanket on the cot. Behind him, he heard Nucci's footsteps strangely light, almost like a child's. Nucci went out and pulled the door shut after him.

## 23

Diane folded the money into her purse. A hundred dollars wouldn't carry Buzz far. Pretty soon he'd be back for more. And she didn't have it, couldn't raise it without going to her father. Griscom would guess right away that she needed the money for Buzz. He wouldn't give it to her without asking a lot of questions. Maybe she should go to him now, make a clean breast of the whole affair.

But she didn't dare. Not until she knew how deeply she was involved. Buzz hadn't killed Dottie; she was sure of that because Nucci had practically admitted the murder to her. But the old caretaker on the Maitland estate was still on the critical list. If he died, what charge could be brought against her? She didn't know, didn't dare take a chance.

This morning the police had identified Dottie's body. To date, they hadn't linked Dottie with Buzz or Nucci. Maybe they never would. A girl like Dottie would have plenty of boyfriends. Why should the police single out Buzz? But she knew she was whistling in the dark. Buzz was wanted already for questioning concerning Belle Foley's death. That was something Diane couldn't understand. Buzz had been with her the night Belle Foley died, except for the time she'd spent alone in the restaurant. Had Buzz gone back to the house where he lived and killed the old woman? Why would he do a thing like that with Dottie lying dead in his room?

She didn't know. But tonight she'd have to persuade Buzz to leave the city. Maybe if he went far enough away, changed his name, the police wouldn't catch up with him. Maybe they wouldn't look too hard. No matter what happened, tonight would be the end for her and Buzz. What if Buzz wanted her to spend tonight with him? She'd been willing enough two nights ago. Why should it be different now? Maybe it would seal the bargain between them, assure his silence. But she didn't think so. A woman's body wouldn't mean that much to Buzz. She'd guessed that from the start. It was part of the fascination that he'd held for her—the wild, unleashed energy within him she'd mistaken for strength. Even then she had known that he couldn't be bound. She couldn't check his headlong flight. She could only run with him or turn away.

As she stepped into the hotel, she saw that Johnnie Lacy was waiting for her in the lobby. Her first reaction was annoyance. Why couldn't Johnnie leave her alone? Then she thought of Iris upstairs. If Johnnie were with her, she could ward off her mother's interminable questions. Iris would like Johnnie, Diane thought wryly. There was something steady, reliable, about him.

Johnnie took both her hands. "Have you heard from Buzz?"

She told of Buzz's visit during the night. Johnnie said angrily, "That's what I'd expect of Buzz. Coming here, dragging you into the mess, demanding money. Next time you see him I'm tagging along."

She didn't answer. She didn't want an argument with Johnnie. She'd find a way of slipping away from him later. Despite her promise, she'd have to see Buzz alone this time.

She had expected Iris to be at home but when she and Johnnie stepped into the apartment, they found it deserted. She turned to speak to Johnnie but as she did the telephone rang. When she picked it up, Buzz's voice came across the wire, low and guarded. "That you, Diane?"

"Yes."

"You got the dough?"

"I've got it, Buzz."

"Solid. Now listen." He gave her the address on 116th Street, repeated it. "You got that, sugar? Okay. The front door'll be open. You go right on up to the roof.

Nobody'll stop you. I'll be waitin' there. You understand?"

"Buzz, does it have to be the roof? Can't we meet somewhere else?"

Anger made his voice grow loud. "What do you think, that I'm going to take the lettuce from you in the street? Can't you understand this ain't no game? We're playin' for keeps. If I get tagged it's likely to mean the chair. I picked the roof because it's the safest place. There won't be nobody around, and in case you're tailed I'll get plenty of warning."

She hesitated. "All right, I'll come."

"You better, baby. And don't take a cab straight up here. Mess around a little. Make sure you ain't followed."

"I'll try."

"The later you come the less chance there'll be of somebody gettin' nosy. Is twelve george with you?"

"I guess so."

"One last thing. Be sure you come alone."

"But Buzz—"

"Don't argue with me, just do like I tell you then everything'll be all right. But you cross me up and somebody's going to get hurt."

She called his name again but already the connection was broken. She stood still, holding the instrument in her hand. A touch on her arm made her jump. She looked up to see Johnnie. She had forgotten he was there.

Johnnie said savagely, "I heard. He wants you to meet him on a roof, smack in the middle of Spanish Harlem."

"He says it will be safer that way."

"It's a trick, Diane. Don't go."

"I've got to."

"You don't have to do everything Buzz wants. Tell him to fly a kite."

"You don't understand. Sometimes you have to do things because—" She stopped, not able to express the compulsion that drove her toward Buzz.

"Well, one thing's for sure. You're not going without me. I'm sticking close."

"I won't let you."

"You can't stop me, Diane. I heard the address, the time. Either we go together or I get there ahead of time and have it out with Buzz. That stud doesn't scare me."

Diane broke away from him and crossed to the window. A block away she could see her mother, walking slowly toward the hotel. She turned to Johnnie.

"Let's get out of here," she said. "Let's get out quick."

## 24

Buzz lingered on the corner in front of the poolroom. Now that he'd put in the telephone call to Diane, he ought to head back for the room Nucci had got for him, hole up there until it was time to meet Diane. The night had turned warm and muggy, after the chill of the last few days. The thought of sweating out another five hours in the tiny, barren cubicle gave him the willies.

He'd like to shoot a game of pool, but with all the cops in town keeping an eye peeled for him that was asking for trouble. But as long as he was moving, he ought to be safe enough. The cops would be combing the hipster hangouts around Times Square, the jive joints on Swing Street, but they wouldn't think of looking for him up here in Spanish Harlem.

He pulled the rim of his hat down lower and swung along, taking it easy. Nobody paid him any mind until he reached 110th Street. He wouldn't have recognized the little punk leaning against the side of the candy store if the stud hadn't started to sidle away, his eyes almost popping out of his head. Buzz did a double-take and the kid almost turned green, he was so scared.

Buzz got his number then. He was one of the jerks who'd done the mugging in Central Park, the guy who looked like Luis and was probably his brother. The kid backed toward a doorway, and Buzz grinned. This stud had been a right bold guy last night when it was three to one but now he was itching to pull a fade.

Buzz knew he ought to pass him by. He had too many irons in the fire to mess around with a punk like this. All the same, the guy had plenty coming to him. Buzz thought of the pointed toe crashing into his ribs last night, of the burning pain along his shoulder.

This jerk was a real dope. He'd boxed himself in the narrow entryway. The door behind was probably locked, and his only way out would be past Buzz. His eyes were liquid with fear and his face had gone soft as a baby's. This was too good to pass up. Buzz took a few slow steps toward him.

"You was a real mean cat last night, wasn't you, punk?"

The kid didn't answer. A trickle of saliva formed at the corner of his mouth. He wiped at it with the back of his hand, then his hand came down quick and Buzz saw the switchblade in it. There was a soft ping as the blade snaked out. The kid was moving fast, the shank held low to sweep upward.

Buzz grabbed at his wrist, caught it and spun him around. He jerked back hard and heard the bone snap. The kid let out a soft moaning cry that changed to a howl. His knife clattered to the sidewalk. Buzz slammed him forward so that his head hit hard against the tiled wall of the entry. The kid crumpled and Buzz drove his foot deep into his stomach. He leaned over, scooped up the blade and turned around.

A little circle of people had formed on the sidewalk. They were talking excitedly, but when Buzz faced them they grew quiet, drew away from him.

If he started running they'd be on top of him, yelling, screaming for the nabs. It wouldn't matter that the kid had pulled a knife on him. These were the kid's people; they'd back him up in any story he'd tell. Anyway Buzz couldn't afford a brush with the police. It wouldn't take them long to spot him as the guy they were looking for.

He acted by instinct, holding the switchblade at his side, walking directly toward the center of the watching group. They pulled away, startled, frightened, uttering muffled little cries. Buzz stopped, looked around. Nobody moved. He walked on rapidly but he didn't run, not until he was across the street and halfway down the next block. A bus had drawn up at the corner. Buzz sprinted for it and swung aboard just as the door was closing. Nobody could have followed him, that was for sure. All the same, the Puerto Rican voices, high and shrill, rising all about him, got on his nerves.

The bus crawled along. If the kid was hip, he could

call his gang together and tail him in a taxi. Buzz knew he ought to get off, double back to Nucci's place. But he couldn't bring himself to leave the comparative safety of the bus. He hunched down low in his seat, hoping nobody could spot him from a passing taxi. He stuck his hand in his jacket pocket and clutched the switchblade he'd taken from the punk. The feel of the warm metal gave him a little confidence. He got up quickly and jumped off the bus at the next stop.

No sign of Luis or his gang. Hell, he'd been imagining things again. He must have broken the kid's arm. They'd probably be rushing him to a hospital now.

All the same, it was a fool's play. He should have left the kid alone. Once these cats had a real down on you, they never let up until they evened the score. From now, on he'd have to watch himself every time he stepped out on the street. He'd shaken them for the time being but it wouldn't be hard to trace him back to Nucci's place.

He wished he'd brought the revolver with him instead of stashing it beneath the pillow on his cot. To hell with it. He had too much on his mind to worry about Luis and his punks. After tonight, he'd clear out of Spanish Harlem for good. He looked around and saw the lights of a Hamburger Heaven. It made him realize that he hadn't eaten all day. Maybe going into the place was taking a chance, but he had to stoke up some time.

He took his hamburger and coffee to a corner, thinking over his plans for the night. The setup wasn't as good as last time, but it ought to work. Nobody was going to blame him for plugging Nucci, not when he caught him red-handed in the act of raping Diane. After that it ought to be a cinch to pin Dottie's murder on Nucci, and the creep wouldn't be around to involve Buzz. From then on everything ought to be easy sailing. No one could ever prove he'd as much as touched Belle Foley. That left Bailey, the old caretaker. He could lay that on Nucci, too, if Diane would string along with him on the deal.

Yeah, Diane was the real problem. How far should he let Nucci go with her? Diane could back part of his story but she could give him away too. Maybe it would be better if she died, like Dottie Marr. No one could have any doubts about Nucci's guilt then. There'd be no one to contradict any story that Buzz might tell. He batted the idea around, weighing its pros and cons. It gave him a good feeling, knowing that he held Diane's life in the palm of his hand. Almost as though he were God. He wouldn't make up his mind now. He'd let it ride, see how Diane treated him tonight.

He ordered another hamburger and ate it slowly, enjoying himself. Things were just the way they ought to be. If Diane acted nice to him, she'd come out of this scrape all right. But if she put on a snooty act like she had in the lobby of the Piermont, then she'd die.

When he left the restaurant, he didn't even look around. He grabbed the first cab that came along and ordered the driver to take him straight to Nucci's place.

He mounted the stairs softly, hoping Nucci wouldn't hear him and stick his head out. He didn't want to yack with the guy. He was feeling high with the sense of power and he wanted to stay that way. A couple of reefers would do the trick, keep him right up on top until it was time to go to the roof.

At Nucci's landing, he stopped to listen, but he heard

no sound. He started climbing again. He got his key out to open his door but when he touched the knob, the door swung open. Buzz straightened up with a jerk. Nucci was sitting on the only chair. His eyes passed over Buzz expressionlessly.

Buzz said, "What the hell is this?"

Nucci raised a big hand, showing the flat palm. "Take it easy, boy. I just got to thinkin' as how maybe you was lonely so I decided to come and sit it out with you until it was time for the trim to show. You wouldn't want no more mistakes like last time, would you?"

Buzz stared at him with loathing. The guy must have been hitting the main line. His pupils were pinpricks, making the slate gray eyes enormous. A spasm of fear shook Buzz. Maybe Nucci had searched the room, found the gun. He went to the bed and flung himself down on it. He felt the hardness of the gun beneath the pillow and breathed a little easier.

He turned to Nucci. "Why don't you broom off? Let me get some kip."

"What's the matter, Buzzie boy? Ain't my company good enough for you?"

There was no sense arguing. Nucci was too high. He twisted around to face the wall. The room was so quiet that he could hear Nucci's shallow breathing, but at least he didn't have to look at the creep.

## 25

Diane sat at a table in the Green Elephant watching Johnnie Lacy's fingers as they ranged the keyboard of the battered piano. His style was tight, controlled, an intricately woven contrapuntal background for the instruments that made up the unit. Vaguely she could sense the discipline, the restraint, the skill that gave assurance and authenticity to the scarcely audible strumming of the black keys. But to her the music had a certain sterility. It lacked the passion, the anger, that poured forth from Buzz's magic hot-rod digits. Johnnie's music spoke the words softly, underlining them, repeating, striving to make the listener understand. Buzz's music was a scream of anguish, the sound of flight, confused, clashing, discordant. It jangled on the nerves like a man hammering on prison bars.

Johnnie had not let her out of his sight since Buzz's telephone call had come through. In a way she was glad. She had scarcely listened as he talked about his theories concerning progressive jazz and the techniques he was developing with his unit, but his presence had helped to fight back the mounting panic which had enveloped her at the thought of meeting Buzz. Try as she would, she could not destroy the image of Dottie Marr's naked, bloodstained body lying on the rumpled sheets of Buzz's bed. Even here, with Wally Jones beside her and Johnnie smiling down at her from the bandstand, it seemed to her that Frank Nucci must be watching her every move with his blank, expressionless gaze.

Nucci wouldn't give up easily. Would he be trailing her tonight through the streets of Spanish Harlem? Or would he be watching Buzz, waiting for another chance to strike? In her mind, she felt the thrust of his knife slicing into her flesh. She shuddered. But she knew she would keep her rendezvous with Buzz. The tension of the last few days had to be broken. She would have to free herself of Buzz and then find Nucci.

Nucci was the creature of a dark and shadowy world, she thought. If she could drive him out into the light, it would be he who would run away.

She forced her attention back to the music. Johnnie was speeding up the tempo and the rest of the band swung in behind him. The trombone arrived, taking over, but the whole unit rode along, building a picture, interpreting a scene. The tonal sentience was beyond Diane's understanding but she was caught up in the mood of throaty defiance that issued from the horn and which was counterpointed by the quivering throb of the drum and the muted notes of the piano.

She looked at Wally and he grinned at her. "The way that unit floats in is killing me. Johnnie's got the educated touch. He can hit like a speed ball, hot and cool at the same time."

The music faded out, with only the trombone riding high to a finish. Diane glanced at her watch. Half an hour to midnight. It was time to go.

Johnnie was walking toward the table. He dropped his hand on Wally's shoulder. "Carlo's switching from the drums to the piano. Can you fill in on the tubs?"

"Sure, why not? But you haven't been leveling with me tonight, Johnnie. I smell trouble. Why not let me tag along?"

Johnnie looked at Diane who shook her head slightly. He said, "Thanks, Wally, but not tonight."

Wally shrugged, moved toward the dais. Johnnie squeezed Diane's hand. "Time to get rolling."

They made the trip uptown mostly in silence but as they approached the north side of the park, Johnnie's fingers tightened around Diane's. "Let me go up on the roof with you."

She bit her lip. They'd argued it out before and he'd

agreed to let her see Buzz alone. She said, "Please, Johnnie, let's not go over it again. If Buzz sees you, he'd be sure I'd given him away. He might panic, do something crazy."

"I don't like it—you on the roof alone with him."

"I've been with him before. Buzz has never hurt me."

"Hasn't he?"

"Johnnie, try to understand. I'm saying goodbye to Buzz. I'm telling him this is the end. I can make it stick. But not if you're there. He won't be turned down in the presence of another man without a fight."

"I don't like it."

"Keep your promise to me. I agreed not to go to Buzz without telling you. But you've got to let me talk to him alone."

Johnnie's lips brushed her forehead. "You win, Diane. But I'm going right up to the top landing. If anything goes wrong, scream. I'll be there fast."

She smiled at him in the darkness. "Thanks, Johnnie."


They followed Buzz's instructions and left the cab two blocks from their destination. Despite the lateness of the hour, the street echoed with sound. The wail of a jukebox flooded out through the open door of a pizzeria. Radios and TV sets chattered through the open windows. A couple quarreled in a doorway.

They found the corner. Pale yellow light splashed onto the sidewalk from the grime-streaked window of a poolroom. A group of Puerto Rican boys clustered around the entrance, dressed identically in black jackets. They were chattering in low staccato voices but they broke off as Diane and Johnnie passed close to them.

The house was near the middle of the block, a dilapidated old brownstone. Diane hesitated in front of the stoop, looking up at the high uneven steps, the rusted wrought-iron grillwork, the narrow door topped by a grubby fanlight. In spite of herself, a tremor shook her body.

Johnnie put his arm around her, held her tight. "Call it off, Diane. Let me take the money to Buzz. I'll tell him if he bothers you again, I'll beat the hell out of him."

"No, Johnnie, it wouldn't work. This is something I've got to do myself. If I don't, it won't be ended. Can't you see that?"

She climbed to the door quickly, with Johnnie close behind her. In the hallway, she hesitated again. A dangling naked bulb cast black shadows beneath the stair well, scarcely lit the splintered wooden steps. The air was stale, heavy. The odors of rancid fat, garlic and marijuana smoke almost gagged her.

Somewhere far above a radio blasted out a program of Latin-American music. Other than that the place was so quiet that it had an air of being abandoned. They started up the stairs, the treads creaking beneath their weight. Half way up the first flight, Diane turned. A movement of shadow caught her eye. A boy had opened the outer door, was standing just inside the hall. From his black jacket she judged he was one of the boys who had been on the corner. He saw her gaze upon him and slipped soundlessly back through the door. The furtive movement added to her sense of danger. But she dismissed the boy from her mind and hurried on.

Her desire to run became almost overpowering. But which way? Upward to Buzz? Or back down the stairs to the noisy street? She wasn't sure. She had told herself that she was through with Buzz. But now that she was so close to him, a yearning for him swept through her. She sucked in her breath. She'd have to hold herself in, give no excuse for Johnnie to follow her to the roof. If he did, Buzz would be angry. The hard core of fury that was never far from the surface might be laid bare, might lead to some fresh act of violence.

She had reached the topmost landing. Narrow, unpainted stairs, scarcely more than a ladder, jutted upward through the skylight. Diane looked at the crooked rectangle of gray sky. Buzz would be waiting for her somewhere up above. His arms would circle her again, draw her close. Was that what she wanted?

The touch of Johnnie's hand startled her. She had almost forgotten his presence. She didn't look at him, knowing that he would plead again to be excused from his part of the bargain. And she had to see Buzz alone, to make certain of what she felt.

Johnnie said, "I'll be right here. If you need me, call. And if you're not back in ten minutes, I'm coming up."

She moved away abruptly, keeping her face averted so that Johnnie might not see the tension and uncertainty there. She mounted the rickety stairs rapidly. The roof was dark, striated by black shadows cast by the chimneys, the coping, the jutting framework of the skylight. The radio in the room below clicked off and in the sudden silence, the distant roar of the city traffic echoed through the night with startling clarity.

At first she thought that she was alone, that Buzz had not come. Alarm sent prickles of fear along her spine. What could have happened to him? Had the police arrested him? Had Nucci caught up with him? Surely he would have kept the appointment unless something had gone seriously wrong.

A soft sibilant sound caught her attention. Then her name was whispered. "Over here, Diane."

She saw him now. He was seated on the low cornice, his back against a rise in the wall, his hands linked about his ankles. His sprawled figure was silhouetted against the gray sky. A tiny circle of red marked the tip of his cigarette.

She had expected him to rush to her, to throw his arms about her, to kiss her. Her reactions would have been the final test. Would she be able to turn from him, remain aloof, or would she be swept away by the emotions she had sought to repress?

She stepped toward him. He did not rise or move until he was only a few feet away. Then he got up slowly and remained still, waiting for her to come to him. His face was in shadow and all that she could see was his shining eyes, the arrogant tilt of his head.

"Buzz, are you all right?"

He laughed harshly. "Sure—as right as a guy can be with a murder rap hanging over him."

There had been other questions she had wanted to ask. But his bitter voice, his hardness, shut her off. She stared up at him without speaking. Gradually she could make out the tight mouth, the hollowed cheeks, the drawn lines of his face.

"Did you bring the dough?"

Her heart sank. Was this all he wanted of her? Was money the only thing that mattered? She snapped open her purse, drew out the roll of bills and handed them to him. He crumpled them into his pocket, his head cocked to one side.

"I been thinkin', baby. A hundred bucks ain't much for a guy on the lam. But maybe you could get your hands on some real lettuce. Maybe a couple of grand. Then we could go off together. Have ourselves a real ball."

"No, Buzz. That's all I've got."

"You could ask Griscom. You could make him shell out if you went about it right."

"He wouldn't do it. Anyway—"

"Anyway what?"

"I won't try. This can't go on."

His fingers tightened on her arm so that she wanted to cry out with the sudden pain. His eyes were blazing. "I thought maybe that's the way it was with you, sugar. You played along just for the kicks. But now the chips are down and things are getting rough, you want out. What does it matter to you if Buzz Baxter gets tossed in the can or fries in the hot seat?"

She tried to wrench free, but his fingers bit more deeply into her flesh. He was bending forward, his face close to hers. Suddenly he was a stranger. His face was a mask of evil. His lips covered hers and she couldn't move away, but a shudder of revulsion passed through her. Even so, in some secret part of her she felt glad. She was free now, free forever from the spell which he had woven around her.

When he straightened, she looked up at him unflinchingly. "You've got your money, Buzz. May I go now?"

He gave a gurgling laugh and his hands fell to his sides. "Sure, baby, sure. Walk right out of my life. But you ain't going far, not as far as you think. Because I got a little surprise waiting for you."

The words were without meaning for her. She swung

away and took two steps in the direction of the skylight before she saw the figure of the man limned against the darkness beyond. There was no mistaking the sloping shoulders, the lean-waisted body, the menacing catlike crouch of Frank Nucci.

Behind her she heard Buzz's mocking laughter. She knew in a flash why he had lured her to the roof. She was to share the same fate as Dottie Marr. She tried to dart past Nucci, but he pounced upon her, his arms circling her like metal bands.

# 26

Buzz stepped back deeper in the shadows. There was plenty of time. He could wait. He knew now what he'd suspected for a long time. Diane would sell him out to save her own skin. She was a threat. His lips twisted in a wry smile as he watched her struggle silently against Frank Nucci. He didn't need to feel bad about her. She'd betrayed him, hadn't she? So she had this coming to her. If Nucci killed her, it was all to the good. If he didn't, Buzz would have to finish the job after he'd dealt with Nucci. So what was there to do but wait?

The revolver was snug in his hand, ready for action when the time came. And at this range he couldn't miss. He caught a glimpse of Nucci's face, the whites of the eyes showing, a trickle of saliva at the corner of his mouth. The goon was crazy, a real psycho. Buzz was tempted to blast him right now. It would be good to watch Nucci die.

Diane's body went limp. Buzz heard the rip of cloth. If he let himself, he could almost feel sorry for Diane—

but that was acting like a dope. In his mind he toted up the score against her. She'd chased after him like a little floozie, hadn't she? Then after she'd involved him in murder, messed up his life so that he was on the run, she had tried to walk out on him. One thing was certain, she couldn't live now. She couldn't be trusted. Especially after the way he'd tipped his hand, letting her know he'd baited the trap for Nucci, that he'd known all the time that the goon was there by the chimney ready to pounce on her. Yeah, Diane's death would cancel out a lot of things. So why should Buzz Baxter shed any tears over her?

Diane slipped downward, sprawled on the crackling tar paper that covered the roof. Nucci was standing over her, a shank in his hand. Buzz caught the glint of the blade. He'd had Nucci tagged right along. He was a creep who got his bangs out of using a knife. Buzz braced himself. He'd have to be careful. To shoot fast and straight. He'd have to get Nucci in a vital spot with his first shot—otherwise the goon might get close enough to use his knife. He stepped forward, angling for position, his revolver raised. But he still had to wait. Wait until the knife plunged down into Diane's body. That was the best moment to shoot. Before Nucci could straighten up.

Running feet thudded across the rooftop. Buzz looked up and saw Johnnie Lacy racing toward him. Suddenly there was no time left. He had to get Nucci before Johnnie reached him. Otherwise he could never make his story stick. He swore under his breath and took a single step forward. His finger tightened on the trigger of the gun.

The shot made more noise than he'd thought possible. The sound reverberated along the empty roof, bounced back from the higher buildings beyond. Nucci had been crouching. He jerked upright, his hand moving toward his chest. He lurched toward Buzz. Buzz danced away, fired again. This time there was only a sharp click. Desperately Buzz triggered the revolver a third time. It was jammed. He slammed it hard at Nucci, heard the sickening spat as it struck his face. Nucci kept coming on and Buzz was backed against a chimney. Nucci's hand shot out, clutching at Buzz's jacket. Buzz ripped free, seeming to pull Nucci forward with him.

Nucci started to fall, his hands spreading out in front of him almost as though he were praying. The fingers closed on air. His knees buckled and he sprawled forward, landing with a jarring thud. Buzz stared at him as though hypnotized. Then he remembered the switchblade in his pocket. He ought to make sure that Nucci was dead. But it was too much of a gamble to take with Johnnie Lacy here on the roof, with lights going on in the houses all around.

Buzz glanced at Johnnie, who was kneeling over Diane. Johnnie looked up and met his eyes. Buzz knew that Johnnie was hip to why he had waited so long in the shadows. Yeah, Johnnie had seen too much. Johnnie was a menace now, as well as Diane. His hand darted to his pocket and his finger caressed the thin blade he'd taken from the kid early in the evening. He closed in on Johnnie, moving surreptitiously, hoping to take him by surprise.

A voice shouted from somewhere not far away. Buzz saw a figure in the house across the street, a woman framed in a square of yellow light. The woman screamed something, the words indistinguishable. They didn't matter anyhow. What was important was that the row would bring the cops. Buzz couldn't afford to be trapped up here on the roof. There were too many things he couldn't explain. Panic took hold of him, sent him scuttling across the roof toward the skylight. He half ran, half stumbled down the narrow stairs to the top landing.

The house was ominously quiet, the doors along the corridor closed. No one here would want any truck with the police. They must have shut themselves in when they heard the shot. He started down the next flight, then checked himself. There was a figure in the dimly lit landing below. He sucked in his breath, then released it again. Only a boy. He was getting scared of shadows. He'd have to cool it, use his head or he'd really conk off.

He took the next few steps more slowly, fighting down the panic, getting himself under control. The kid stood still, waiting, just in the crook of the stairs. Another boy moved out of the shadows, stood beside the first. A third came up behind them. There were other footsteps moving quietly, furtively along the narrow corridor.

Buzz shouted, "What do you want? Who are you?"

The first boy looked up and the dim light of the corridor caught his face. Buzz didn't need an answer. He knew now. It was Luis Mercado.

He'd never get down the stairway, not without a knife between his ribs. But there was another way of escape. He'd checked on it this afternoon. Despite the welter of fear that engulfed him, he felt a little glow of self-satisfaction. He was a guy who worked out all the angles, prepared for every emergency. Now his caution was going to pay off.

He swiveled about, started racing back up the stairs.

The house next door was separated from this one by a narrow entryway, not more than three or four feet wide. The roof was a few inches lower than the one above him. From the cornice it would be an easy jump. Once on the neighboring roof, you could move about for almost half a block. You could work your way through a maze of skylights, chimneys and copings until you had a choice of a dozen ways to the street.

He could hear light footsteps on the stairs below him, and shouts, but he didn't need to worry about Luis and his bunch of punks. They'd never catch up with him. But what about Nucci? How badly had he been wounded? Could he be waiting beside the skylight? It was a chance Buzz had to take. Speed was what mattered now. Keep on running. Don't stop.

But he slowed up when he reached the skylight. He came up into the pool of light with his switchblade open. He looked at the spot where Nucci had fallen. Nucci wasn't there. The thud of his heart ripped at his chest and his breath burned his throat. His eyes darted along the roof. Johnnie Lacy knelt just where Buzz had left him. He was holding Diane close. But where was Nucci?

He saw him then, leaning against the chimney. The deep shadow almost concealed him. Buzz might have missed him altogether if it hadn't been for the tiny scrabbling sound that he made. Buzz knew he ought to keep moving, that pretty soon Luis and his gang would be on his back. But the sight of Nucci paralyzed him.

Nucci stirred, straightening himself up; his hands showed gray against the black wall. Then with a groan he propelled himself forward, stumbling toward Buzz. Buzz could see the gray face working, the mumbling lips, the wide-open eyes. Nucci took two weaving steps, then stopped, balancing himself. His hand slid into his pocket, came out with the switchblade. Buzz heard the tiny ping as the spring released the blade.

He should have moved in quick, taken the guy before he could pull himself together, but he'd waited too long. He couldn't stand up to Nucci; not even when the guy was wounded. His hands were trembling and his knees were water. A sob wracked his body.

Foot beats on the stairs. He couldn't just wait for the trap to spring. He leapt to one side. As he did so, Nucci stumbled closer, one hand outstretched like a giant talon. Buzz sprinted for the cornice, not daring to turn. Nucci was after him. How could the dragging footsteps move so fast?

The piercing wail of a siren from the street below deafened him, cut out every other sound. Only a few feet to go, then a leap to the next roof and he'd be safe. One more step, then swing himself to the cornice. That was all he had to do. Something caught at his sleeve, held it hard, jerking him about. He cried out with fear, tried to yank himself free. Who was holding him? Nucci? Luis?

He looked dazedly across the roof. Nucci was still half a dozen feet away, teetering toward him. Behind him was Luis. He saw the rusted iron hook now. It was caught in the torn tweed of his jacket. He'd seen the hook earlier, warned himself about it, but in his panic he'd forgotten it.

He jerked at the sleeve, trying to rip himself free, but the fabric wouldn't give. He threw himself forward, heard the tear of the cloth. Then he was falling, face down, against the coping. His chest took the brunt of the fall. The concrete surface knocked the wind from him. He was sliding forward over the low cornice into the chasm between the two buildings. One leg dangled over the edge. He rolled, catching at the rough concrete with his fingers, clinging, but he couldn't check the forward plunge of his body.

His fingers tightened and his legs threshed beneath him, seeking some toehold to help support his weight. A figure loomed above him. For a moment he looked up into Nucci's gray face, saw it distorted into a vicious grin, saw the gleam of triumph in the slate-gray eyes.

Nucci didn't move. He didn't have to. Buzz's grip was weakening. His fingers spread out, spurting blood at the tips where the concrete rasped the skin like sandpaper. He made a final effort, flattening out his palms, trying to lift himself. His body inched upward, then his hand slid across the solid surface and there was nothing to grasp. He arched backward and his mouth opened in a shriek. Then he was hurtling down, down, into the black void. The police siren wailed again, drowning out his screams, shutting out the sound as his body crashed into the rubble-strewn areaway five stories below.

## 27

Diane lifted her head. Arms cradled her. She struggled fiercely, silently until she recognized Johnnie Lacy's crouching figure.

She sat up then, staring about the roof. She saw Nucci propped against the chimney, then Buzz emerging from the skylight. Johnnie clutched her to him but she pulled free in time to watch Buzz's precipitate flight across the roof, with Nucci shambling after him with incredible speed. Buzz fell and she saw his legs flailing as he tried to stem the forward rush of his body. Then mercifully Nucci blocked her view, shielding her from the sight of Buzz clinging desperately to the coping.

The siren down below wailed like a banshee. She turned and when she looked back Nucci stood at the roof's edge, peering down into the black chasm. There was no sign of Buzz. Nucci drew himself up, twisted about and staggered toward them. For a moment Diane let Johnnie hold her close and buried her head against his shoulder.

Johnnie dragged her to her feet and stood between her and Nucci. The big man advanced slowly, raising his legs too high, teetering, balancing himself as though dancing some grotesque jig. He was a dozen feet away when he stopped and a shudder passed through his gaunt frame. A knee buckled beneath him and he slid sideways. His arms flapped like broken wings. He tumbled forward, his face striking the surface of the roof. He tried to rise, pushed himself part way up, then fell again and lay still.

A searchlight slanted upward from the street, slicing the darkness with its beam of yellow light. Shouting voices and the thud of feet on the stairways below made a wild cacophony of sound. Diane looked toward the skylight. The boy whom she'd seen in the hall when she had entered the building was there. As she watched he ran silently across the roof, jumped to the low cornice not far from where she had last seen Buzz and leapt to the roof beyond.

The first of the policemen arrived a moment later. His service revolver in his hand. He stared about him, saw Nucci's fallen body and played his flashlight across it. Then its beam picked up Johnnie and Diane. He called out coarsely to a policeman who had come up behind him.

Johnnie said softly, "Stay here. I'll talk with them."

He walked slowly across the roof. Diane heard the policeman ask, "What gives here? Hey, what is this?"

Johnnie's answer was too low to carry to her. She turned her back, staring into the night, too numb to feel anything yet. Then Johnnie was beside her again. He said, "The police say to wait downstairs in the prowl car. Can you make it, Diane?"

She nodded and crossed the roof with Johnnie's arm about her. A policeman preceded them, pushing back the few curious bystanders who had made their way into the halls. He led them down the stairs and across the sidewalk. He opened the back seat of the car, watched while they entered, then sat stolidly in front.

Johnnie held her hand and she was grateful that he did no more. At first. they sat in silence, ignoring the prying stares of the crowd which was gathering rapidly on the sidewalk. Then Johnnie leaned close. He whispered, "They'll question us, Diane. We've got to tell the truth. All except that you went with Buzz to Lymington."

She nodded and laid her finger across Johnnie's lips as a warning to be quiet. A second officer was moving toward the car. He stuck his head in the window: "I got to take you kids down to the precinct station. A guy from the D.A.'s office will want to question you."

Johnnie said, "Sure."

The policeman growled, "Sure, what?"

Johnnie didn't answer and the man circled the car and slid in behind the wheel. As the car slipped away from the curb, Johnnie started whispering again.

"They'll have to permit us the use of a phone. Let me call Willis Griscom. He'll come or send a lawyer."

"No. Please, Johnnie."

"They may make things rough for you."

"I don't care. I won't have my father in this. I'll face it alone. It's got to be that way, Johnnie."

"You sure that's what you want?"

"I'm positive."

Johnnie shrugged. She was grateful that he didn't argue.

At the station, she got out quickly, climbed the shallow stairs. A matron took her in charge, accompanied her to a washroom where she cleaned up. The matron helped her pin together the ripped blouse, chatting with her as she did so. Diane remained quiet. She was thinking hard. Johnnie was right. If both Buzz and Nucci were dead, she was safe. But she mustn't let the police know that she'd helped Buzz dispose of Dottie, that she was in the Ford when it struck the old caretaker on the Maitland estate. She was free, she thought, and despite her weariness, a flame of exaltation crept through her. She was free of her fascination for Buzz, free of the threat from Nucci. But more than that, she was free of her mother's soft domination, free of Willis Griscom. She saw the matron's eyes upon her and dropped her own, staring down at her shoes. She still had to be careful. There mustn't be a slip now.

The matron led her to a bench outside an office. There was a long wait; then Johnnie came out. Johnnie tried to come to her but the matron shook her head and moved between them. Diane entered the office. A man sat behind a desk piled high with papers. She had expected her inquisitor to be stern, harsh, but the man was smiling. He stood until she was seated.

She asked quickly, "Is Buzz dead?"

He nodded.

"And Nucci?"

"He'll pull through, I guess. But if Lacy's story checks, maybe Baxter was the lucky one. Nucci'll die in the chair."

Tears sprang to her eyes, but she didn't know why. She felt no grief for Buzz. Only release from the mounting tension of the last few days. She made no effort to hold back the tears but even while she wept, she watched the man opposite her. She saw his face soften. He stood up and came around in back of the table and put a hand on her shoulder. He spoke gently.

"You've had a bad time, Miss Griscom, but it's all over now. We'll need your story and there's a chance you'll have to testify against Nucci in court. But we'll make it easy for you—easy as we can, Miss Griscom."

She looked up quickly at the slight emphasis on her name. He knew who she was, then. Johnnie must have told him. She saw the concern in the man's face. And she understood. It wasn't pity or compassion. It was concern that he might offend Willis Griscom's daughter. She fought back a titter of laughter. She could tell this man anything she wanted and he would believe her, because he wanted to believe her.

She had thought that speaking of Buzz would be hard, but as her words came, it was almost as though she were talking to herself. Pieces began to fall into place and she examined each one with growing detachment. Buzz wasn't real. He never had been. He had been a symbol of revolt. A symbol of flight, of despair. And now that he was dead, the symbols were broken. There was no more reality to him than there was in the harsh, jangling, angry jazz music that had flowed from his fingertips. When the strident dischords had faded away, that was the end. Until you struck up a new note and the music started again.

When she had finished her story, the man went back behind the desk and sat facing her. He said quietly, "That wraps it up, I guess. With your statement and Johnnie Lacy's, it ought to be a cinch to convict Nucci of Dottie Marr's murder."

He hadn't asked any questions, she realized. He hadn't tried to trip up Willis Griscom's daughter. That wouldn't be smart. He added almost apologetically, "Of course, we'll need a written statement, but I guess you're too tired to make it tonight."

She shook her head. "I want to get it over with."

"Sure. I can understand that."

He called in a police stenographer and Diane repeated her story. She waited until it was typed, then signed the document without reading it.

The man helped her up. "It's late. I'll have one of the boys take you home."

"Please, no."

He grinned. "My error, I forgot about Lacy. He's waiting." He had opened the door and she could see the open doorway at the foot of the stairs where Johnnie stood talking to a uniformed policeman.

She started down the stairs slowly. Johnnie didn't see her until she was on the bottom step. He swung about, coming toward her with his arms open. "Diane, are you all right?"

"Yes, Johnnie. But I want to ask a favor."

"You bet. Just call the signals."

"Get me a cab, Johnnie. Then let me go home alone."

His face whitened and she saw the hurt in his eyes. For a minute she thought there'd be another argument. Then he said, "Sure, baby, anything you say."

She let Johnnie brush her cheek with his lips as he helped her into the cab. He closed the door and she settled back in the darkness. Tomorrow, the next day, she'd have to tell Johnnie she was through. He'd take it hard. But it would be better that way. Johnnie was another cord binding her to the life she didn't want. Buzz had taught her one thing—you had to be ruthless with people like Johnnie, like her mother, like Willis Griscom.

As the taxi sped downtown, she leaned forward and directed the driver to take her to Times Square. She didn't know where she was going, but she wasn't going home tonight. She had cut herself loose from the past but the future was still a maze. Somewhere in the flashing lights, the glaring brilliance, the bedlam of sound, she would reenter the world of the hipsters. But now she would be more certain of herself. She wouldn't need Buzz. She could find her way without him.

She stepped out into the surging crowds of Broadway. She stood still for a few moments staring up at the huge flickering signs high above her. Then she began to walk, slowly at first, then faster and faster. She lost all sense of direction, but she did not stray far from the bright lights. Music flooded out into the street. She could hear it while she was still half a block away. A horn broke loose, spreading heady raucous defiance into the night. It rose higher, shriller until it seemed that it must burst. She stopped in the shadows to listen. The music died suddenly, leaving only the sounds of traffic, laughter and voices. She held her breath until it started again.

The savage rhythmic beat built up quickly. A woman's voice, too high-pitched, wailed a dirgelike melody, the words slurred and meaningless.

Diane took a step toward the music. Someone moved beside her and she realized she had not been alone in the shadow. She did not look at the man but waited for him to speak. His voice was hard, self-assured. "You look lonely, baby. What's the matter? Did the boyfriend stand you up?"

She gave no sign of hearing him.

"Hey, don't put on the high-hat act, honey. I just been thinkin' any stud that would pass up a sweet piece of candy like you must have rocks in his head. But why be lonesome? There's plenty of fish in the sea. So come on, let's get close. Let's have a ball for ourselves."

She turned slowly, looking him over. He was tall and lean. His dark face was hard, the flesh tight against the heavy cheekbones. He looked a little like Buzz, she thought, only bigger, taller, stronger, more sure of himself. He wouldn't run as quickly as Buzz. Fear would come more slowly. But flight was in him too. He would be dangerous even as he ran.

Excitement threaded her thoughts. She began to walk rapidly along the dark street, hearing the man's footsteps match her own. She kept her face averted but when he touched her arm, she did not move away. She would never go back, she thought, and smiled a little to herself. Meanwhile she had a fit companion for the night. Tomorrow maybe there'd be someone else. It didn't matter. In flight you were never alone.


## THE END

Wenzell Brown Bibliography
(1912-1981)

*Crime Fiction*
Murder Seeks an Agent (Five Star/Green, 1945; Arcadia, 1947)
Run, Chico, Run (Gold Medal, 1953)
Gang Girl (Avon, 1954)
The Big Rumble (Popular Library, 1955)
The Naked Hours (Popular Library, 1956)
Tomboy Jungle (For Men Only, 1957)
The Wicked Streets (Gold Medal, 1957)
Teen-Age Mafia (Gold Medal, 1958)
Teen-Age Terror (Gold Medal, 1958)
Prison Girl (Pyramid, 1958)
Witness to Death (Saint Mystery Library, 1959; et al)
Cry Kill (Gold Medal, 1959)
The Hoods Ride In (Pyramid, 1959)
The Rum and Coca-Cola Murders (Saint Mystery Library, 1960)
The Murder Kick (Gold Medal, 1960)
Bedeviled (Monarch, 1961; stories)
Girls on the Rampage (Gold Medal, 1961)
Jailbait Jungle (Belmont, 1962)
An Act of Passion (Monarch, 1962)
Women of Evil (Monarch, 1963)
Sherry (Monarch, 1964)

*Historical Fiction*
Dark Drums (Appleton-Century, 1950; Popular Library, 1951)
They Called Her Charity (Appleton-Century; reprint as *Devil's Spawn*, Perma, 1952)
The Golden Witch (Monarch, 1964)

*Science Fiction*
Possess and Conquer (Warner, 1975)

*Non-Fiction*
Hong Kong Aftermath (Smith & Durrell, 1943)
Dynamite on Our Doorstep: Puerto Rican Paradox
  (Greenberg, 1945)
Angry Men—Laughing Men: The Caribbean Caldron
  (Greenberg, 1947)
Introduction to Murder: The Unpublished Facts Behind
  the Notorious Lonely Hearts Killers (Greenberg, 1952;
  reprint as The Lonely Hearts Murders (Signet, 1952)
Monkey On My Back (Elek, 1954; Popular Library, 1954)
The Violators: Stories of Criminals from the Files of a
  Veteran Probation Officer of the Bronx County Court
  (with Israel Beckhardt; Harcourt, 1954; Popular Library,
  1956)
They Died in the Chair (Popular Library, 1958)
Women Who Died in the Chair (Collier, 1963)
How to Tell Fortunes With Cards (Bell, 1963; Paperback
  Library, 1971)
The Kept Man (Lancer, 1964)
The Kept Woman (Lancer, 1967)
The Promiscuous Woman (Lancer, 1967)

**Wenzell Brown** was born on May 10, 1912 in Portland, Maine. He obtained his master's degree from Columbia University in 1940 and went on to teach at schools in Puerto Rico and China. His first book, *Hong Kong Aftermath*, published in 1943, was based on Brown's

experiences during the fall of Hong Kong. He then began writing hard-edged juvenile delinquent crime novels for publishers like Gold Medal and Popular Library. Brown also wrote true crime works and won the Edgar Allan Poe Award from the Mystery Writers of America for his 1958 work, *Women Who Died in the Chair*. In later life he returned to his teaching career. Brown died in December 1981 in New York City.

www.ingramcontent.com/pod-product-compliance
Lightning Source LLC
Chambersburg PA
CBHW050510160726
48003CB00001B/241